The Long Years

The Long Years

Lauran Paine

Thorndike Press • Chivers Press
Waterville, Maine USA Bath, England

This Large Print edition is published by Thorndike Press, USA and by Chivers Press, England.

Published in 2001 in the U.S. by arrangement with Golden West Literary Agency.

Published in 2001 in the U.K. by arrangement with Golden West Literary Agency.

U.S. Hardcover 0-7862-3395-8 (Western Series Edition)
U.K. Hardcover 0-7540-4599-4 (Chivers Large Print)
U.K. Softcover 0-7540-4600-1 (Camden Large Print)

The text of this Large Print edition is unabridged.
Other aspects of the book may vary from the original edition.

Set in 16 pt. Plantin.

Printed in the United States on permanent paper.

British Library Cataloguing in Publication Data available

Library of Congress Cataloging-in-Publication Data

Paine, Lauran.
    The long years / Lauran Paine.
      p. cm.
    ISBN 0-7862-3395-8 (lg. print : hc : alk. paper)
    1. Dakota Indians — Wars — Fiction. 2. Large type
books. I. Title.
PS3566.A34 L65 2001
  813'.54—dc21
                                    2001027606

Contents

Preface

This is a fictional novel and no claim is made to authenticity. With the exception of the last and final chapter, it follows closely the actual theme of the early days in the American West — the time of the first serious hostilities between the United States and the mighty Sioux (Dakota) Nation.

The names of the majority of Indians herein were those of actual warriors of the times, but one must remember that Indians frequently changed their names after a victorious battle, or subsequent to some great event, so that considerable duplication must necessarily occur. This confusing practice has led many readers and students the world over to a common error in identification.

So — the Indian names in this story were borne by proud and valiant warriors of a hundred years ago, although, with a few exceptions — notably Colonel Harney

— the white men in this story are all fictional.

The battles occurred too, except for the final one. Conquering Bear lived and died as shown, as did many of the other great fighting men of the Northern Cheyennes and the Dakota Nation. It is to the memory of these people — still grossly misunderstood and still well aware of a departed greatness — that this book is dedicated.

LAURAN PAINE.

Chapter One

ONE OLD COW

He could stand up straight with the wild musk odour of his body around him and see the world — his world — radiating out from him in all directions — like a splayed out splash of Universe with himself as the centre of it. He was a Dakota; a great Dakota. But he stood with his heart on the ground and it wasn't to feel the vastness of his world running out from his body that he stood thusly.

It was because he was hungry and his people were hungry and his horses were hungry. The Dakota people were waiting for their special White Man to come and hand out the annuity goods the Indians received every year for keeping the peace and not fighting or killing or plundering. The leaves of autumn, the blades of grass, the minnows in the streams, that were the white people, straggled forever across Dakota land, going somewhere westward

9

and never returning, littering the plains with their worn-out animals, their broken down wagons, and their pitiful graves. That was what he was waiting for and that was what his people were waiting for.

Broken Hand was dead. There was a new White Man Father coming to them. He was coming, but when? Winter wasn't far off. Babies looked out of coal-black eyes at mothers who couldn't make enough milk and the horses looked like drum-heads — the skin pulled too tightly over their skeletons.

The Dakotas waited. The last days of the warm hunting season were passing like golden seconds dipped in delay. But they were to wait, so they waited. The warrior stood there with the late afternoon sun cooling him, thinking how it was that a Dakota warrior — a Sioux fighting man — could stand like that and feel the land of his people running out of his body in every direction. It was thus because the Dakotas were proud and mighty and valorous and had kept their land for themselves until just lately when the white people had come in herds. The Dakotas were still great and mighty and fierce, but some things had changed and this was one of them.

He looked down the road that was a

ribbon of scabs over the land, studying its farthest distances. He saw nothing that would be the White Man of the Dakotas except a lone white man afoot driving a tottering old cow. Every once in a while he would catch the wind just right and hear the curses of the walking man without understanding anything but the tone of voice. So he watched the strange spectacle thinking to himself that white men were strange. They would drive one old cow like that; a cow so old and burdened with her years that she was worthless, and beat her along with a thick club going toward the West. Always toward the West beyond — some vague place Westward.

It wasn't understandable — driving old cows and not riding a horse — any more than most things the white men did. But he stood there watching because the man and the rickety old cow were all that moved along the twin scratches that were the white man's wagon ruts. When the man with the cow was close enough, he saw him glancing with vast misgivings at the big Sioux encampment. And that was humorous, for, while the white men always were afraid among the Red men when they weren't in numbers, there wouldn't be any trouble. Broken Hand, Tom Fitzpatrick, sometimes called White Head, had seen to that when he sired the peace treaty that said Dakota land should belong to the Indians "for as long as the grass shall grow. . . ."

The herd boys were bringing in the Dakota horses. Like all boys of quick blood, they brought them in from the far grazing in a rush, howling simulated war shouts, riding like miniature warriors and looking the part. The Dakota watched and smiled. He wasn't old. Not too many years ago he had done the same thing, trying hard to impress the people with his horse-manship, his tawny strength. It was a quick moment of reflection and he dwelt on it, still watching.

The white man and the old cow were abreast of the camp and the boys — like all boys before and since — veered over to make a mock feint at him. That was under-standable too, but the old cow, goaded to exasperation by her drover's club, threw up her tail, let out a wild bawl, left the road and went charging across the little distance and into the Dakota encampment. With her tongue lolling spittle and her sunken eyes showing the whites, she careened in among the tipis and scattered the screech-ingly indignant squaws from their cooking fires. The half-wild dogs were set in a frenzy of excitement while she tore the side out of a lodge and sent warrior shields and lances, planted before their owner's tipis, into the dust. Bawling hoarsely and tearing through the bivouac, the Dakotas watched her in surprise. Even the herd-boys hauled back on their single rope rein and sat there astonished, feeling uneasy over what they had caused.

The encampment was alive with angry howls from the enraged old women and suddenly the Dakota saw Straight Foretop snatch up his rifle, toss it to his shoulder and fire. The racket subsided gradually and the camp returned to normal.

The Dakota turned and looked back where the white man was. He was standing stock still, close enough for the glistening, oily look of his sweaty face to be visible. There was shock and fear stained into his expression. While the warrior watched, he turned and ran. The words he cried out were muffled and unintelligible, but a fighting man who has seen and heard fear at other times, recognises it anywhere in any tongue.

The white man was fleeing like an old woman and shouting out in a way that was fear-prompted. The Dakota watched him in vast surprise. He was safe. More than that, he could have had a good horse from Straight Foretop's herd for the killing of the old cow. That was still tribal law. But the white man became small and he was still running. It puzzled the Dakota, and he turned his head away from it. It made him feel ashamed to see a grown man run like that, whimpering and deranged with fear. He looked back up the trail. Where was their White Man, their Indian agent who would come and distribute their annuity goods? The people had eaten everything there was to eat. He turned swiftly and glanced toward the bivouac. There was a delicious smell in the air of roast meat. He swung toward the encampment and smiled a little. The old cow, of course. Well — that would hold them another day and by then surely the White Man would come. He strolled slowly back toward the camp. The herd-boys were busy with the horses; more busy than ever. He understood that childish wish to be too busy for the oldsters to scold them. Well — they'd get scolded, but on a full belly a man can endure certain indignities, and boys can endure even more. He walked on, following the wonderful aroma . . .

14

★ ★ ★

Boone Helm heard the story of the breathless, greasy-faced man three times, and yet the man never told him the story, personally, even once. He just happened to be at the sentry's post beyond the walls of Fort Laramie when it was first reiterated. That time it was recited with the most haste and the least embellishments. He had listened where he'd stood against the mud wall feeling the warmth going into his back, and paid no especial attention. One old cow.

The second time was at the sutler's wagon and that time it was more graphically, more indignantly told. By then the Indians had stolen the cow and maybe even chased off its owner a little ways down the road. Boone had looked with quiet amusement at the ring of faces, seeing the dry grins the other scouts and oldhands had passed among themselves while the blue-clad soldiers took it all in.

But the third time, when it was repeated by the soldier officer, he failed to see any humour in it at all.

"They surrounded him and took his cow and swore they'd kill him if he didn't run all the way to the fort. Then they laughed and paced him with their horses, waiting

15

for him to drop so's they could lance him."

The soldiers swore heatedly and savagely. Indians — gawdamned Indians — always the same thing! Boone Helm listened to the talk and drifted away while it was at its height, walking in his heavy flat-heeled boots, scuffing the dust of the dry, summer-baked ground, looking down.

"What's all the fuss?"

Boone glanced up a little. A tall, old man — at least he had the appearance of age from the criss-crossed lines in his face and the watery blue of his eyes — was hunkered at the corner of a soldier's building, smoking and nursing the little triangle of shade he was squatting in. Boone looked at him thoughtfully without speaking, then he drifted closer and dropped down. The older man gave way a little although there was ample room for them both in the shadow.

"Some pilgrim was driving his cow out past the Dakota camp. Cow got away somehow and ran through the In'yun village and got shot."

"In'yuns shoot it?"

"Yeah. Funny thing is that when this pilgrim first came panting up to the fort he said the cow had run away and the In'yuns killed it when it was ransacking their village. Next time I heard the story it was different."

"Sure," the lean, aged-looking man said, running his eyes over the soiled, dusty, interior of the place, seeing and unheeding all the men across the compound. "What'd ye expect? That's the way things get started. Man drops a rock on another feller's toe. First it was an accident, then it wasn't no accident, then pretty soon it turns out he's plannin' ways to break this other feller's toe for years." The light blue eyes swung and glanced at Boone Helm's profile. There was a sour little wisp of laughter in their depths. "People're like that. I reckon they always will be."

"Well . . ."

The bugle call was clear and clarion-like in the dry air. Boone Helm never finished what he was going to say. Instead he and the bony man beside him sat relaxed and watched the soldiers stand muster. It was always interesting to see. The thin line of them, cavalrymen and walking-soldiers, blue — deep blue — their faded uniforms dyed nearly their original colour with man-sweat; and red faces above. Men with inherent independence in them could always watch the unison of soldiers and marvel at it and feel a pinch of contempt too. Like buffalo calves, those blue-bellies. Wherever their mothers went, then they went too. When the old cow turned aside on the trail to bypass a rock, the calves did the same.

The older man knuckled back his flat-crowned hat and his forehead was almost indecently white in contrast to the weather-red of his ancient looking face. He made a pipe-load of red-bark sputter to life until the sting of the smoke was around them with a tangy, wild savour, then he spat aside and spoke again, holding the little pipe inches from his face with both hands.

"Where's their darned agent? Ain't wise to leave 'em settin' out there like that. They'll wait until there's no grub left, then they got to eat something."

Boone Helm spoke absently, listening to the snap and snarl of men's names and their whiplash answers as the muster was called. "Like this cow. Well —" he shifted position on the hard ground, "it's bad anyway. The soldiers don't know and won't listen. The pilgrims listen and repeat it ten times worse, like this cow-man has."

The bugle started up in a thrilling, yet sad call. There were a few blanket-Indians within the confines of the parade but not many. Not since the fort passed from private hands to Army hands. Indians weren't allowed inside much any more, except a precious few. Boone watched their dark faces and wondered what they saw in the white man's pomp and ceremony. They'd love it although they wouldn't understand any of it. Why? Because they loved any kind of ceremony and were great for it and had so many intricacies of their own that they walked in a maze of taboos and entanglements of the mind that they were forever observing. He mused that it was odd — these people with their fierce freedom and quick resentment of encroachments — and they weren't free at all. They had saturated themselves with idiosyncrasies and ceremonials, with visions and dreams and visions so complex that they dared do nothing until their medicine and medicine bundles said it was right to do it.

The soldiers were dismissed and the long, wonderful twilight began. The older man knocked out his pipe, pushed the dottle around with one scuffed boot-toe, and settled back again.

"You want to ride out there, don't you?"

Helm shrugged. "I wasn't thinking that."

"No? Well you would've before long. I know you."

Helm's smile was a slow expression that

lingered. It was still around his eyes and mouth when he answered. "We know 'em — the soldiers don't. They got Lucien Fontenelle to interpret. He can't speak enough Dakota to spit on, even if he's sober enough to do it. We could go out and tell Conquering Bear he'd better get in here and pay for that cow before the Army goes out there and somebody gets hurt."

The other man grunted, said nothing and pushed around among the dead pipe ash with a stubby, dirt-ingrained forefinger. He was thinking of the ride out and back. It wasn't that he especially objected. He just thought it was foolish is all, riding out there, talking, then riding back.

"Ready, Parker?" Boone Helm got up and squinted with a half-smile at his friend, dusted the seat of his britches and regarded the other man's resigned look with almost impish amusement.

"Ready as I'll ever be."

They rode out westerly. The sun was sinking like it always did over the Laramie plains; slowly, reluctantly, like a man dies who is full of interrupted life; stubbornly.

"Grattan's got his wagon guns all ready again. Pretty fiery feller, Grattan."

Boone nodded slowly, looking into the sunset. His face wasn't handsome except in the serene look it had. The eyes were too deep and the nose a mite thin, flaring out at the nostrils. His cheekbones were high and prominent and his mouth was good-sized but thin-lipped, which emphasised the redeeming feature of a well-moulded chin and jaw that had a dogged, abrupt sweep to it. There was that calm, perfectly confident look to the face that struck men right off. It was hard to describe; rather more inherent poise than anything else.

"Mitchell's head man, Parker. Grattan can't do anything unless he's told to."

"I know. Well — nothing'll come of it anyway. Just a damned old cow. The Bear'll give a horse maybe, or maybe he's even got another cow somewhere among the tribes. He'll make it right."

Helm didn't speak again until they came within sight of the ghostly upright triangles that arose with unearthly eeriness up out of the prairie. Boone saw without looking and knew without thinking, which tribes and sub-tribes were there. Brulés and Minniconjous and Oglalas visiting their kinsmen, and an occasional Northern Cheyenne lodge. The Northern Cheyennes were more than the allies of the Dakotas, they were almost their brothers. They would rise up with their friends — and go down with them.

They were challenged, more, Boone got the impression, with hope than with curiosity. He answered the sentinel, telling him he had come from the white man's fort to see Conquering Bear. It was enough. They were passed through.

The village had eaten but no face showed satiation. The gloaming made a diorama of the bivouac. Dogs ran at will; lean, slab-sided animals with sly eyes in heads held low and canted a little, watching the white men pass, bristling a little at the peculiar, tame odour of them. The children stared up from around the dying fires as did the people, but none moved. It was like riding through a forest of bare sounds that whispered and clucked rather than sounded. Riding past wet, black eyes that stared at them impassively but intelligently, showing nothing but their blackness. There was a smell, too, a stench rather, of nomads encamped too long — far too long — in one place. Then they were at the large tipi with the bottom rolled up to catch a stray summer breeze off the earth. The lance stand was there but the shield was covered with its buckskin sheathing. Boone ducked around it and entered. Parker followed after handing their reins into the hand of the tall Dakota who had loomed up with a grave, reddish face and held out his hand for them.

Conquering Bear listened gravely. There was the ironclad etiquette or he might have interrupted them, for he had already been in to see the white officer, Mitchell, and explained about the cow. But he listened to Boone and when he finished, told him about his visit, spreading out his hands and looking almost apologetically like he had at the white officer.

"The man ran away from his cow. He was afraid. We made meat of her. The treaty says we must settle differences with the whites in peace. I went to the white officer. We talked. He gave us molasses to eat and coffee and we talked. I went to settle this cow in peace."

"And?" Boone asked softly, feeling a tightening somewhere behind his belt.

Conquering Bear's little look of deferential affability faded. "Grattan used strong words. Flemming did too. Wyuse interpreted badly. Some of us know a few words too. I was told I must send in the man who shot the cow. I can't do it. He's a visitor. He has a guest's rights. Besides, he is a Minniconjou of the northern people and I am not their leader."

Boone and Parker sat there stony-faced, listening. Parker's mind was mulling over this eternal difference between men. Red skin or white skin; all had ten toes, ten fingers, two eyes. Why was it always the same? An obstacle planted so firmly between them they would never come together. Why?

But Boone Helm thought of something else. One old cow. Even one good, fat, young cow — or two cows or ten cows. It was no cause for trouble, and yet he had a feeling behind his belt buckle that more than a dead cow taken and eaten by a patiently waiting — and just as patiently starving people — was going to make something come of all this ridiculousness. Men — especially Red and white men — had leapt at one another's throat for less, but *his* race was the wiser. They should know better but they never did; never. Maybe neither race was very smart then, for even coyotes wouldn't fight over one bony old carcass, tough enough to make moccasins out of.

". . . sixty horses. He could take his pick. Or Straight Foretop himself would give the owner of the old cow two of his best horses. More, if he has to. We do not want trouble over this. We are a hungry people. Where is our agent? Where are our annuity goods?"

Boone let his breath out slowly. "I don't know. The longer I live the less I know."

"Hau, hau," the Dakota said with a wry nod. He knew how a man came to say things like that all right. He thought it himself very, very often. It was so. Wisdom was supposed to come with age. It did once, but not any more. Now there was bewilderment piled upon bewilderment. "Hau," he said again.

"What came of your council?"

The Bear was long in answering. His dark face was averted a little. "Soldiers will come tomorrow. I am to give up Straight Foretop."

"Does he know it?"

"No. How can I tell him? I'm not his leader. He is a tall reed and a strong one. He is a warrior. He won't go."

"You sure?" Parker asked.

Conquering Bear's glance shifted. "He won't go," he repeated with a quick, clenched fist gesture.

Boone sat in the silence and felt a weak coolness stray in under the rolled up bottom of the lodge. They all sat like that for a long time then Boone arose and took

Parker with him. They went out into the night, got on their horses, said *"Pila-mayaya"* to the buck holding their horses and started back. A thing as big as all the night to Parker Ellis came out of him like blue-green bile and spilled down from his mouth and fell into the stillness unbroken except for the dull, dusty, clop, clop, clop of their horses's hooves on the wagon road. Rancour —; despairing impotence in the face of fear and hatred. His words dripped it. His bearing was steeped in it, and he prefaced what he said with terrible oaths that made the younger man look at him.

"I've trapped from the Missouri to the Green and from the Sacramento to the Canadian with Joe Walker. I seen the beaver go and the late-comers roll in. I seen the goddamned trails trashed over with busted thunder mugs an' the creeks littered with filth. An' I seen a whole damned world fall apart, Boone, just like that." He made a slashing motion with one hand, flat and palm downward.

"I fought Crows in their damned Absaroka an' Snakes an' Pawnees an' 'Rickaris an' even what's left o' the Mandans. An' the Lord above us knows I fought Sioux from hell to breakfast, but by

God — hear me boy — I hate what's happenin' now. Hate it so's it makes my guts sick inside me. There's the Bear — his lance stand an' his skin house an' his — oh, what's the use o' talkin' about it! There's no good in it, Boone. It makes me sick inside myself. There they are, not allowed in the fort or the white man's dirty little villages, a-sittin' out there waitin' for a feller who doesn't give a damn whether they wait until doomsday or not — and they don't know it's like that. They really believe their treaties. They don't know their White Man don't give a tinker's damn for 'em — even hopes they *do* starve to death. Now this. This business of an old cow. Where's the end o' it, Boone?"

The younger man didn't answer. His chin was pushed out into the night ahead of him, his profile was steady and hard and expressionless. Parker Ellis had lived a long time. Sometimes Boone thought those old ones had outlived their time; not their usefulness but their time. They had a bitterness in them that was exactly the same bitterness the Indians had, but didn't know it. They'd fought like mad-men to wrest this land from the Indians and hadn't really won. Now they were seeing it taken from them in turn. It was the same bitterness, the same terrible resentment. But he didn't say anything and let Parker get it out into the open and cleanse his mind of it. The old-timers and the Indians both, were hanging around unable to leave, seeing a fresh young earth, a bountiful wilderness, vanish, and they couldn't get away yet. They were chained there until their hearts stopped.

They had to stay and witness an awful destruction. Boone understood. He had come late to the mountains, but not too late. He was seeing the last spasms. He didn't like it either, but it was different with him. The yesterdays weren't so long, so full of wonderful things. He thought of the tomorrows. Ellis didn't.

"What'll the Army do, Boone? Say something — man. Don't ride along there like a damned Flathead."

Boone spoke, understanding Parker Ellis. Men together for a long time know one another very well. Even know their thoughts sometimes and surely the way they react to different circumstances. Boone wanted words to draw the depression out of him.

"There are a lot of them, Parker. Oglalas, Brulés — a big herd of them and they're all warriors underneath. Dakotas 're the best fighting Indians I've ever seen. The Army won't walk softly because it doesn't know how. You know that just like I do. The Army doesn't know Indians either. They're animals to be killed — we've both seen that attitude too. Well — they might send out to get Straight Foretop like Conquering Bear says, but I'll give you odds they don't take him. I'll lay you a bet they just won't get him."

"What'll happen, then? They'll fight, Boone. I'll tell you what'll happen; they'll fight."

But Boone shook his head. "The Bear's wise, Parker. There won't be any fight. He'll keep 'em held down."

"They'd better not tie into them In'yuns, Boone," Ellis said savagely, as though he wished with all his heart the Army would — and that's exactly what he wished and how he wished it. "They'd just better not. There's The Bull Who Resides Permanently Among Us, there's Gall and Red Cloud an' the *akicitas,* the soldier societies. There's all of 'em, boy. Like Smoke an' Crazy Horse an' Little Hawk the Cheyenne, and Lord, that's not scratchin' the surface. There's all the Siouxs, the Minniconjous, the Brulés, the No Bows an' Hunkpapas an' Blackfoot an' Two

29

Kettles an' . . ."

"I know," the younger man said softly, hearing in his pardner's voice a softer note that meant the end of the storm was nearing and it was safe to interrupt now. "Let's veer off here and go over to Barlow's place."

Parker Ellis squinted across in the darkness, then reined his horse northward off the road into the warm, velvety blackness that was buttoned down hard at the farthest corners of their world. Brooding, he rode for hours like that, beside Boone Helm, moving unconsciously to the rhythm of his mount, silent, like an Indian would have been. Parker was an Indian. A White Indian. He wasn't the first against whom the environment had rubbed and wouldn't be the last.

With his deep-set eyes feeling the night for a candle flicker that should be off to the north, Parker filtered the atmosphere through his mind like an Indian would have done. The instinct for peril was strongest in those who dwelt with death and atrocity. It became like an Indian's instinctiveness was; so acute everything, even the blackest night or the shape of a cloud or the sound of the wind, had a meaning. Then he grunted and Boone Helm saw it too. They rode toward it unaware that gradually the pale flicker shone off their faces and made them evil appearing.

Boone swung down near the conical little mound of prairie hay within the round corral and tied up. Tugging off his saddle he dropped it on the blanket, slid off the bridle and watched the horse shake himself. He faced the still night and the black square of the log and sod house, waiting. When a man materialised, he was lithe and high-headed with a great shock of unruly chestnut hair that shone dully in the watery light of a late moon.

"Howdy, Tyre."

"Hullo, Boone. Hullo, Parker. Come on in."

"Was you a-bed?" Parker Ellis asked.

"Naw. Drinkin' coffee. Come on."

They went in. The candle light was mellow and wonderful. It made the night outside, a foreign world. Boone Helm's eyes moved only a little bit but it was all there in his glance — the washed furniture of pine and fir, the black fireplace, the smell of food and civilisation. The cabin had an odour all its own — as different from an Indian camp as night from day — softer, more blunted and less tangy. Standing by the great oaken table, tall and lithe and with the same tawny chestnut hair and deep blue eyes, was Tyre Barlow's sister, Jane. Boone's eyes held to her face, drank it in and refreshed his memory, touching up the image from the original, that was in a private place in his mind. She turned away, reaching for two more tin mugs that hung from pegs. He could see the outline of her body as she turned. The long, supple sweep of it had strength that was packed under the handsomeness. It made a tightness settle around his heart, like a big fist, squeezing.

Parker was talking to Tyre. The words filled the room with their acidity. Boone heard but paid slight attention. It was the story of the old cow and he was beginning to be sick of the making of a mountain out of a molehill.

Jane Barlow flashed him her quick smile, dropped her glance and nodded toward a chair. He sat. They all sat and played with their coffee until Parker was finished, then each crawled into his own world and sat there without moving, turning things over in their heads. Boone looked across at Tyre. The big blue vein at the side of the Kentuckian's neck was throbbing with a slow, heavy cadence. It could have been anger, but when Tyre spoke aloud his voice wasn't edgy.

"Wait a minute, Parker," he said. "I know how you feel. I know why you feel that way. A man studies things that're dangerous to him. I don't know as much about In'yuns as you two do, but I know a couple of things. I got to know them because I live out here away from the fort, so I know what's likely to happen. I don't like In'yuns, but I don't hate 'em. They got good and bad just like we have, but I'll tell you boys what I think, and then you'll know why I stay out here waiting for the day when I can farm without guns and knives hangin' all over me and stayin' within sprinting distance of the house." He made a motion with one hand toward the high, narrow windows, too small for a man's body to squeeze through. "And to live in a house instead of a fort." He finished speaking without looking up from contemplation of his coffee cup. "When they made that Treaty of '51 all of us who'd been out here for a spell knew it wouldn't work. In'yuns live by fighting. They always have and you boys know it. They get their dignity, their horses — everything — from fighting. They live with weapons on 'em all the time. They hunt with weapons an' can turn into a fighting man just by altering their target a little. An In'yun has only his tribesmen as his friends. He lives by warring."

"Just take the Dakotas, for instance. They've always fought the Assiniboine, the Blackfeet, the Crows, Comanches, Flatheads, Crees, Shoshones, Pawnees — and us, the white men. That's just the Sioux. All the tribes are like that. There's no such thing as peace among any of 'em, an' there never has been. They live by hunting and by fighting. They've got to. That's their way. Treaties be damned. If you take away their hunting places an' kill off their game — which is what's happening right under their noses — an' don't give 'em a substitute in the way of food, then they got to fight to get fed — don't they?"

Parker Ellis drained his cup and set it down squarely, looking over at Tyre Barlow. "I ain't sayin' they don't have right, Tyre. What I'm sayin' is that there's goin' to be trouble — an' over an old gummer cow — that's what I'm sayin'. I'm also sayin' that the Army don't know beans about In'yuns."

Parker flopped back in his chair with a brooding, scornful look. "An' what's Lieutenant Mitchell got at the fort? Fifty soldiers an' his wagon guns. Tyre — you know how many Dakotas are out there? Well — there's around five, six hundred lodges of 'em. That means better'n a thousand fighting bucks."

"What soldiers are at the fort?" Tyre asked.

"Sixth Infantry," Parker answered with the scorn in his voice unabated. "An' we went over to see *Mato-wa-yuhe,* ol' Conquering Bear. He told us all that I told you afore. So there it is, an' mark me, Tyre, Lieutenant Grattan said he could lick the Sioux nation with ten good soldiers, an' all the Plains In'yuns with thirty."

Jane Barlow looked up at Boone. "Did he, Boone?"

The heretofore silent member of the little group nodded. "Yes, he did. I was there with Park. What makes it worse, Jane, is that he really thinks he can."

Tyre swirled the dregs in the bottom of his cup. There was a dogged, stubborn look to his square, wind-burnt face. "Well — we'll still stay out here. I've fed 'em and counciled with 'em often enough."

Boone's shoulders moved as though tightening up against a blow. He leaned on the table as Jane went after the big pot again. "Listen, Tyre. This isn't the same. If Grattan goes after that Minniconjou who shot the old cow, they'll fight him. They'll fight, man, because they're starving to death, eating their moccasins already, and winter isn't even here. They're desperate. You can hear 'em chanting their death songs when you ride into the camp. It's a frightening thing, Tyre. They're so close to the edge that one little push, one more insult, will do it. If they take up the hatchet, no one'll be safe. No one at all — and that means you too."

Tyre Barlow's head was still low, his gaze sombre and stubborn. He said nothing and didn't have to. The answer was there in his face. Jane poured out more coffee into the tin cups then sat down again and looked across the table at Boone Helm.

"Will it come to that?" she asked quietly.

He cupped both hands around the cup and felt the warmth in his palms. "Maybe. Parker thinks so. The Army doesn't, of course."

"Are they going to send men after the warrior who shot the cow?"

Boone nodded. "Yes, we heard that from Conquering Bear. That's what made me ride over here tonight." He swung his glance to Tyre's brooding face. "To tell you to at least go to Fort Laramie for a couple of days. Make a trip for supplies — anything — but go in an' stay for a day or two until we see how the wind's going to blow. Will you do that, Tyre?"

"There haven't been any important skirmishes since the treaty, Boone. This is summer, '53. Almost three years. It may come. I believe they'll fight all right, like I said a while ago, but not now. Not this time. And if they do, they've got strong ideas about friends. I don't think," he concluded slowly, thoughtfully, "we're in much danger." He glanced up, saw Boone's look of near anger, and dropped his glance again. "Oh — a few'll ride past with warpaint on 'em, but we always see some like that. What the devil — we all know the chiefs can't control the soldier societies."

"It'd only take one *akicita* man to kill you, Tyre," Parker Ellis said bluntly. "One bullet for you an' one for Jane."

Boone drank his coffee. "Let Jane go then, Tyre," he said. "Don't make her stay here after what we've told you."

"They'll fight, like I said, but not this time. I feel it in my bones."

Parker Ellis made a wry face. "I've seen a lot o' bleached bones o' men who guessed wrong. Lots o' 'em."

Boone shot him a dark look. Parker flushed and looked embarrassed and avoided the girl's glance at him. "Well — I don't like nothin' I've heard or seen today. Nothin'. There's times like that, fellers. You ever notice it?"

Jane Barlow smiled understanding at the old trapper's tactful withdrawal from a delicate position. "More coffee, Parker?"

"No thanks, ma'm."

"Boone?"

"If you're going to."

"Tyre?"

"Reckon not." The brother got up and looked over at Parker Ellis. "Come on, you boys'll stay the night. Let's put your horses up."

They left the room and Boone was abruptly conscious of a sudden blanketing awkwardness, of magnified self-consciousness, that came out of the shadowy corners and settled thickly over everything. Even over himself and the handsome girl across the table from him, with her eyes downcast, stirring her coffee with a horn spoon. His throat was dry too, and he was speechless when she raised her glance and looked him straight in the face. The candle light was reflected in her look. It was a soft, gentle expression and something else he couldn't define, but it was beautiful like she was, to him.

"Boone — is it that bad, really? I mean — isn't Park just wrought up like he gets now and then?"

"He may be, Jane, but it's as bad as we've said. Why do you think we rode way out here?" He leaned forward a little, staring intently at her. "Listen, Tyre will let you go to Laramie tomorrow. Saddle up and go. Wait a day in town an' see how the wind's blowing."

Her smile remained but she shook her head very slightly and very slowly, back and forth. "What about Tyre? He'd be alone if they came — wouldn't he?"

There was no answer to that. If Tyre wouldn't go, then his sister wouldn't either, and if neither would go, then Boone must hope he and Parker were wrong. A man can only do so much. He slouched in the chair and felt tired. Actually it was defeat in his undertaking with the Barlows that made him feel that way more than personal exhaustion.

"Boone?"

He glanced up quickly at her. Her head was a little to one side and he could see the candle light imprisoned in the red-gold of her thick, curly hair.

"Why don't you stay over with us for a few days?"

"Wish I could, Jane. We've got to meet a train at Laramie an' guide it to Fort Bridge. Otherwise we would."

She studied his face, still holding her head a little to one side. She had always liked that peculiar aura of confidence and calmness about him; the look he had of being thoroughly capable — but kindly and thoughtful as well. He was good looking like a strong man is good looking without being handsome, and she'd been impressed with that two years before, when she'd first seen him. He was the kind of a man a woman came to love; not the kind most women would fall in love with at first sight. Jane admired and liked him.

"Do you know Lieutenant Grattan, Boone?"

"Know him? No, not exactly. I know him to nod to is about all. He's new out here an' he doesn't like In'yuns, I can tell you that, an' he's pretty quick-tempered. Wyuse, Lucien Fontenelle, has told him about In'yuns." His eyes lifted to her face. "You know Wyuse, Jane?"

"Only by sight and what I've heard of him."

"Well," he mused, "that's enough. Half-breed Iowa, an' mean. Drinks like a fish. If it weren't for his dad being a trader with influence, I don't think he'd last long. He can't speak enough Dakota to be a good interpreter anyway."

"It's things like that, that worry you and Parker, isn't it?"

He made a rueful little smile at her. "Well — they help," he said. "But there are other things, like Tyre, for instance. He sits here and tells us why the In'yuns will fight again, then he turns right round and refuses to go on to the fort, when he's just said. . . ."

"But Tyre doesn't mean they're going to fight tomorrow or the next day, Boone. He means they'll fight someday, because it's their nature."

"That's exactly what I'm saying, Jane. It's their nature an' they're being forced into it, no matter how or why, it still amounts to the same thing. And I say they're going to fight within the next week; the next day or two maybe, depending on what Grattan does out there at their camp. Not just someday, but tomorrow, Jane." He saw the tolerant expression on her face and threw up one hand. "You're as bull-headed as he is."

She laughed at him and looked up when her brother and Parker Ellis came back into the room.

41

Chapter Two

SEARCH

Now came a day from which one could start counting time. It was a beautiful summer day with lots of warmth and light in it and lots of people walking everywhere. Some going one way, some another, and some, like 2nd Lieutenant J. L. Grattan, riding to an unknown rendezvous with destiny, at the head of thirty soldiers from Fort Laramie. Two wagon guns, so-called because they weren't emplaced and stationary, but with wagon wheels under them, were pulled along cumbersomely by horses.

The dust rose up from behind Grattan's little column. It was the tell-tale, cursed signal that plagued all travellers over the plains. Indians relied more on the dust-banners than anything else to acquaint them with the coming of others. So the dust rolled up lazily, dun-brown and heavy, and Grattan's infantry rode in wagons behind which toiled the two wagon guns.

Grattan was new in the land; a West Pointer with zeal and scorn, with contempt and disdain in equal parts. He was a powerfully built, stocky man who knew nothing of Indians and despised them and their barbarism. He knew nothing either, of Indian warfare, but he would learn. . . .

The sun was sliding off the meridian when the column came up over the landswell and stopped there, looking down into the great, wide valley that sheltered a splash of primitive colour. Below him were hundreds of Indians. The camps were scattered and the ground around was bare of horse feed and littered with the refuse of a nomad camp too long in one place. There were lance stands with owner's shields of bull-buffalo hide, thick enough to turn a bullet, planted firmly before the tall lodges. There was colour and movement such as few have ever seen, and neolithic pageantry aplenty. But there was hardly any noise at all. It was as though the Dakotas were fearfully waiting. Not cowed, but afraid without knowing why, which was the worst kind of fear to a deeply religious and superstitious people.

But fear didn't destroy caution either. The squaws were taking down the lance stands, working the tipi pegs loose in the ground for easy withdrawal, in silent, sombre haste. The Oglalas rode by on their way to witness the coming of Grattan for they had had word that he was coming and in what strength. The Minniconjous and Brulés waited, wooden-faced. Old men, wise and thoughtful, talked. Conquering Bear was among them. Lazily the early afternoon ticked off its minutes as the blue-bellies came creaking and bouncing down the prairie toward the encampment.

When he was close enough, Grattan called out in a thunderous voice. No Indian answered or came forward. Many sat their horses like statues, watching. After all, many weren't of Conquering Bear's people. They were only bystanders. To the soldiers they were Indians, that was all that mattered. Grattan got red-faced and cried out again and again. He got back a huge slice of silence. Then he turned to the 'breed called Wyuse. "Ride in and call out Conquering Bear. Tell him why we are here. Tell him we want Straight Foretop and no delay. Right now!"

Wyuse rode in and yelled out his denunciations, his profanity and his hatred, for he despised the Sioux and always had. The Brulés came to life. Warriors appeared bearing the tools of war and women and children came next. They moved stealthily among the forest of tall tipis and disappeared toward the breaks along the river. Conquering Bear came up, and far behind the soldier column came more Sioux, Oglalas, riding slowly and bunched up, their heads turned and eyes fixed on what was happening ahead of them. Scattered tribesmen of every sub-tribe converged on the troubled spot where Conquering Bear was gesticulating, and red-faced Grattan, spoiling for trouble, sat his horse.

There was They-Are-Even-Afraid-Of-His-Horses and Big Partisan and High Back Bone (called Hump). A host of men, not so close in were stripped down to their breechclouts putting on paint symbols and winding up their hair in tight clubs. But Grattan had eyes and words only for Conquering Bear.

"Fetch him out here," Wyuse interpreted in his bad Dakota. The Bear sent a runner, but Straight Foretop wouldn't come. He sent back word that he would die where he was, and for Conquering Bear to take his people away so the fight wouldn't spread. They could all hear a death chant somewhere in the near distance but paid no attention. The chiefs were erect and proud, but supplicating, in their blankets. Grattan

45

spoke angrily to Wyuse. The Iowa 'breed repeated it to the Bear, who immediately sent the word to Straight Foretop again. The answer that came back was simple and eloquent.

"The whites have killed both my brothers. I have seen what happens to the Dakotas they put in their iron house as prisoners. I am strong. I am not afraid to die but I don't want to die over one old cow. I will give a horse; two good horses, for the old cow. I don't want the Brulés blamed for this. I will not go into the little iron house. I am strong with my weapons and they will not take me away alive."

Conquering Bear offered horses from his own herd as did others of the Brulés. Lieutenant Grattan stuck to the letter. He wanted Straight Foretop and no damned stolen Indian horses. He stared at tall, fearful old Conquering Bear for a moment, then swung his red face and barked an order. The soldiers snapped up their arms and fired a volley into the Dakotas. Conquering Bear's brother jumped into the air and fell threshing. Blood was running out of his mouth and ears. The headmen ran then, all but the Bear. He yelled for the Dakotas not to fire back. The white soldiers had first blood — they would be satisfied now — the cow was paid for.

Straight Foretop came racing from his lodge with his rifle in his hand, howling into the bedlam that grew as Grattan ran to his wagon guns and aimed one of them, shouting orders to his sweating soldiers. Conquering Bear's voice was lost in the abrupt howl that went up from all the Indians. Some Oglalas, back behind Grattan's men on the white man's road, stopped in dumbfounded amazement when the first volley was fired, then they too gave the yell and kicked out their horses. By then Lieutenant Grattan had yelled for another volley and fired his wagon gun. That time the Indians were over their initial shock and fired back. Conquering Bear went down with one leg bent grotesquely under him; the ragged bone-ends protruding. One arm was shredded flesh and through the middle part of his torso another big slug had ripped its way. He would die, but not yet.

Grattan's cannons thundered and shook the earth. They smashed lodges flat and sent great flapping pieces of decorated hide in every direction, making havoc of the nearest tipis.

There could no longer be anything said or done that would hold back the Sioux

47

fighting men. They came, many astride and more afoot, charging with kill-fierce cries in their throats, and the smell of much blood in their nostrils. They charged into the little band of soldiers while some swerved off and dragged Conquering Bear out of the path of the Red cavalrymen. The soldiers stood for a moment, then broke and fled. All but one little group that stood its ground and was swamped, hacked and shot and stabbed, lanced and clubbed into unrecognisable pulp.

Those who fled ran smack into the oncoming force of Oglalas charging wildly up from the road. They were impaled on Dakota lances and shot down and ridden over. Straight Foretop had deliberately and unerringly shot and killed 2nd Lieutenant Grattan. The Sioux then counted coup on his carcass until there wasn't enough left to identify him by. Spotted Tail was in the forefront of the warriors. He screamed with the voice of an eagle, leading the warriors until there was nothing left to shoot at. Those who fled, the Oglalas systematically butchered. Not a soldier was left alive.

Wyuse — Lucien Fontenelle — had jumped away from his shot horse and fled desperately into a sacred tipi where a dead chief lay in barbaric splendour. Normally he would have been accorded sanctuary there. Not now — not today with the ground slick and scarlet with Dakota blood. The maddened fighting men ran in and dragged him out. He fell to his knees and screamed for mercy but the Sioux flung him down into the dust. Then his brother-in-law went forward and smashed him in the face with a wrong-ended rifle taken from a dead soldier. He fell forward on his face.

No Dakota, regardless of his anger, would accord the fallen man the honour of scalping for he was a bad man and a coward to them. But they tore away his clothes like they did the others from the white man's fort, and made deep knife slashes from his ankles to his hips, severing his tendons so that his spirit couldn't chase the Dakota spirits who had died in the fighting, on their way to the Outer World. Many warriors counted coup on him. They struck him with their weapons and lanced his carcass and stabbed him, but they wouldn't take his hair.

And there it was. There would be no peace on the Platt nor in the uplands, nor upon the plains for forty years yet to come. Blood would flow every day, somewhere.

That was the day to count time from. Wherever Broken Hand, Tom Fitzpatrick was, he must have looked down and felt his blood leak out of him, for all the peace he had striven so hard for, was now no more. The Indians had finally revolted. Tom Fitzpatrick's heart must have been on the ground for all the fine resolve was washed out with Grattan's blood. Now, from a thousand campfires in the stillness of the night, rose up keening chants of sadness for the dead and for the loss of peace, and for what all knew was ahead.

Conquering Bear lived until his skin was pulled taut over his bones and his eyes were sunken so far into his skull they were almost fixed without movement. When he died, the Dakotas buried him in the traditional way. Rolling the great man in his blue blanket, they laid him to rest on a rawhide-lashed platform atop four high, stout poles set into the ground. Tied up there with his weapons and his greatest treasures, out of the reach of the coyotes and wolves, he could see the blue sky above and the traditional home — the rolling endlessness and the flat space — of his people's land where the frontiers were marked with the graves of their warriors.

So the Sioux Wars began; the final wars

fought by the United States against their greatest adversaries on the continent. Not the last enemies they would fight, but surely the greatest, for the Indians would win every battle and lose the war.

"The Grattan Massacre" awoke a muscle-flexing young nation overnight. News-papers everywhere raged against the 'sav-ages' but the fact that Grattan had exceeded his orders and his authority made no difference. Just as it made no dif-ference that it wasn't really a massacre of unarmed men. The soldiers were fighting with wagon guns, long knives, rifles, car-bines and pistols. You can kill a man but so long as he is fighting with weapons he cannot be massacred.

The turmoil raged and the Dakotas struck their several camps and straggled away leaving the fly-blown, naked bodies where they lay. Neither Fleming or Mitchell at the fort would send out burial details because they were afraid to. The trader, Bordeaux, was hired to go over and bury the soldiers.

It was summer and not only was the ground like granite, it was also very hot. Bordeaux covered his face with rags and loaded the bodies onto an old, stiff hide he found, and using his horse, pulled the corpses to a shallow dry-creek, dumped them all in and piled rocks over them. It was a burial of sorts and he collected his money, and thus ended the affair of one old cow. The soldiers were dead, their equipment taken, the Dakotas were gone, the wagon guns destroyed, and the Fort Laramie soldiers locked up their redoubt and wouldn't come out.

Boone Helm and Parker Ellis were inside the fort waiting for a caravan of emigrants they knew now would never come. They heard the news from Crow Indians who related it with much relish. Later, they heard it again. There was nothing else being talked of within the confines of the fort. Parker looked around at his friend with an accusingly bitter, savage little smile.

"There it is," he said, "just like it should've been. Just exactly as any idiot knew it would have to be."

Boone said nothing. There was nothing to say. There had already been too much said anyway. He walked to a parapet stoop and crawled up, with Parker Ellis beside him. Together they looked over the land but always came back to a certain direction and stared that way. Boone was thinking of the slouched, dogged way Tyre Barlow had sat, toying with his tin coffee mug, admitting the Sioux would fight but not believing it would be soon. And Jane. . . . He turned a little to glance at the fierce, brooding profile of Parker Ellis. "You didn't see Tyre or his sister inside, did you?"

Parker swore. "Of course not. They wouldn't come in — you know that. She wouldn't if he wouldn't, an' he said he didn't think it'd amount to much."

"Well — maybe the Sioux won't stay around. Maybe they'll head upcountry. I'd guess they'll go to the Running Water. If that's so then Laramie's pretty safe and maybe Tyre an' Jane are too."

"Hell," Parker said morosely, "you know better, Boone. Don't kid yourself. Maybe part of the tribe'll head for Running Water. They got to go somewhere an' hunt because now they know they won't get no annuity goods an' they got to have winter grub, but you know better'n to say they'll all go. The warrior societies'll be hangin' around here like buzzards, waitin' to catch some poor fool outside his soddy or on the road. From now on a man'll ride this country with eyes in the back of his head. All that uncertain peace is over now. Fight?

From now on there'll be nothin' else."

"All right," Boone said sharply, "how about Tyre and Jane? Do we sit in here like the Army, scairt to death and afraid to open the gate, or do we go see if we can't help 'em get into the fort?"

Parker's look of bleak thoughtfulness didn't alter any, nor did he look around from a slow contemplation of the still land as far as he could see.

"Hoppo," he said in Dakota. "Let's go."

They went, but not until Boone had hot words with the soldier at the gate. They had to get permission from the commander of twenty soldiers — all that was left — to go outside. Even then the Army was drawn up with guns levelled until the gate was made fast behind them. It brought a loud exclamation of scorn from Parker; a resounding insult that matched the look on his face. The Army took it without comment because no verbal lashing could match the terror they felt over this other thing.

Boone laughed harshly as they went across the scuffed ground to less trammeled grass country. His eyes were never still now. "They've been hating and scorning In'yuns for years. They wanted to fight 'em. Now look at 'em. Scairt stiff."

"They aren't very many soldiers, Boone."

"Then why'd they start a war?"

There was no answer to that. Parker lapsed into his brooding silence again. They rode at a fast walk, rarely speaking but always watching, sniffing like a wolf sniffs for danger, studying everything around them, knowing perfectly well that warriors of the *akicitas* were out there somewhere, looking for plunder and scalps; waiting for the unwary, tasting the alkali-ash taste of hate in their mouths and wanting white blood to appease it and wash it away.

The day was hot and the distances swam a little. Trees and sage looked like they were several feet above the ground, not growing out of it. But it was the stillness, the vacuum-hush, more than anything else that hovered over everything. Even to men who had known the Dakotas as friends, there was spine-chilling fear in the hot atmosphere that made the backs of their throats taste like acid.

Friendship was a tenuous thing when race and blood and abysmal differences of belief, and thought, were involved.

Parker had a practical thought. "Now those pilgrims won't come an' we won't get bean and salt money."

Boone shrugged. "I hope they don't. Darned if I want to take their cussed train across to Fort Bridger now. We'd never get there, let alone need salt and beans."

"No," Parker said, "you're right."

"Don't worry, we'll eat."

"I'm not worrying. It's just that I figured to get some new things with that money." Parker laughed off-key. "But — I'll get 'em anyway now. Pick 'em up here an' there more'n likely."

Boone lifted his arm scarcely hearing, and pointed. "What's that — yonder?"

Parker puckered his glance against the reflected sunsmash off the cured grass. "I got an idea. Lone rider, maybe."

They rode toward the distant speck, unmoving and out of place, that looked dark and flat against the vacantness of the dead plain. Boone grunted once when they were close enough to swing down and walk ahead of their horses, studying the ground before they rode over it. It was obvious what the grisly object was anyway, so they read the tracks as they approached it.

"Second blood!"

Boone ignored the words and stopped by a frayed sage bush. "There's blood on that."

"Here too," Parker said, "right in the moccasin tracks. He must've been ready for bear. Couldn't have been the same buck. Must've been two of 'em."

"How many do you make?"

Parker's eyes were squinted up again. He sucked in his mouth and considered before he answered. "Five, six, maybe."

Boone nodded. "Yeah." They stopped and gazed at the battered horse with the man lying behind it with his head on his arms. There was nothing but a red froth where his hair had been. He was dead and tufted, like a porcupine, with war arrows. His guns were gone, and his legs were split from calf to waist, but, oddly, his clothes were still on him. The horse was down with no signs of threshing. His coat still showed wet places although most of the hair was sweat-dried.

Boone spoke aloud to no one in particular, as though to fix the sequence of what had happened in his mind. "Jumped him a long way from here — northward. He ran for it; maybe his horse wasn't stout enough. One of 'em got close enough to set the critter a slanting shot in the brisket. He went down right now an' the feller forted up. Look — most o' the arrows are slanting backwards. They didn't try to

57

smoke him out. Just rode around pumping shafts into his back. He put up a damned good fight."

Parker Ellis grunted. "He maybe killed one or two. He sure as hell hit more'n one of 'em. Shafts look like Oglala but they aren't all the same either."

"Brulé and Oglala," Boone said. "Well — we can't bury him. No time an' no tools. Let's go."

They swung up and rode past with hardly a glance back. Riding with the slanting rays of the lowering sun, blood-red and immense, off on their left, Parker finally spoke.

"Man's got to be crazy to do what we're doin'."

"What d'you want to do — leave the girl to get her hair made into a war-bridle?"

"Naw, o' course not. But gettin' there'll be the easiest thing. Gettin' back'll be harder."

"We'll do it tonight. They don't fight in the dark."

"And what if Tyre won't come?"

Boone turned his head and held the older man's glance. "He'll come," he said quietly, "if we have to beat him senseless and tie him across a horse. He'll come all right — damn his stubborn heart. I'm not going to make this trip again."

"Good. I was worrying about how you'd figured it. Tyre's stubborn as all hell. I like him, y'understand. I think he's first-rate, only he's so blamed bull-headed sometimes. If he don't change he isn't going to be above ground too long. Like I told him the other night. It only takes one bronko warrior to kill a man. They all aren't friendly and even the ones as are, won't put too much medicine in friendship with whites, now."

"The thing I'm wondering," Boone said after a long interval of silence, "is whether they might've gotten there before us. They know Tyre and Jane are out there."

"Well — we ain't wasted much time."

Boone didn't look around when he answered and therefore Parker couldn't see the strain in his face. "That one they scalped back there came from the east, Parker. They're either up there, or they've been around up there. That's what I was thinking. I don't like it."

Parker's eyes moved constantly in furtive little jerks that left no section of the near-distance neglected. He was thinking what he didn't say. It was what they both knew very well. He knew Boone was bewildered, hopeful and fearful about Jane Barlow, and

59

how the younger man was crawling with unsavoury imaginings that could very easily be true if the Dakota raiders had struck the Barlow claim. He cursed Tyre Barlow under his breath and to himself, calling him everything he could think of in passable English, bad Spanish, and barely understandable Dakota. If anything had happened to that girl, Boone Helm wasn't going to be fit to be around for a hell of a long time. He spat with extreme contempt and returned to his grim study of the dead space they rode over.

And it was like that, with his head forward, the chin slamming into the heat as they advanced, that he saw the pile of stones off to their left near some scraggly trees on the edge of a dry creek-bed. Boone was already reining toward the cairn, but that time he didn't get down until they were right up beside the thing, staring at it. Dropping his reins, he walked up to the edge of the rocks and looked at it a long time before he bent and methodically began pushing the boulders away. They fell back into the creek-bed with dull, solid sounds. Parker got down and helped. Before too long they had part of the dead buck revealed. After that they only had to move a few more rocks and there he was, lying flat, face up and a big black stain over the entire front of his war-shirt.

"Shot in the lungs," Boone said. "A wonder he lasted that long." Then he bent lower and studied the man, raised up and began to turn very slowly on his heel, studying the ground. "They rode back and forth here."

"Sure, to hide the tracks." Parker didn't say any more because he saw the revelation coming over Boone's face.

"It wasn't the same band though. Look — they came from the north. They're their tracks. They ran into trouble up there some place sure as the devil." Boone let it slide off, that last word, and he stood there looking into the lengthening shadows in the direction they were headed. Then he looked again at the dead Indian and spoke as he moved toward his horse. "Brulé. Let's go."

Parker's brow was stormy as they kicked their horses into a lope and held the gait for miles. When the animals caught their second breath, they reined back to a kidney-slamming trot and rode like that for a time before pulling them down to a walk. It was hard to see the tracks of the Indians now, but neither of them had any doubts any longer. They didn't even try to read the tracks. It didn't make any difference how many Sioux were in the war party. All that mattered was whether Tyre's fort-like home had proved itself or not.

Boone thought back to the first time he had seen the Barlows. It had been almost two years earlier when the brother and sister were living in their worn out wagon while they laboured like slaves building a home on that big chunk of claim Tyre had bought from the Indians. He remembered thinking what a strange place to make a home, so far from the fort, and yet the country around was open and flat too, so they couldn't be surprised. Still, it was a reckless thing to do.

Later he'd ridden by several more times and finally he stopped and visited, drunk coffee and talked a little, feeling abashed before the steady look of the girl and getting away from it by letting the brother show him the place.

It had taken a lot of work to build that house but Tyre Barlow was a solid, shrewd builder. For all his contrary beliefs about the Plains Indians, he had nevertheless put windows in his house too high for a bowman or a rifleman to be able to shoot down into the rooms and too narrow for a hostile to squeeze past. The walls were as nearly Indian proof as the walls of Fort Laramie. He used mud for his roof so he couldn't be burned out. Then there was the oaken door made at much cost of sweat and groaning. It was thick and massive enough to repel attackers. Two people could hold the Barlow house against an army. It was the only thing that consoled Boone as he rode through the late twilight, forgetting to watch ahead like Parker was doing.

But the Sioux were crafty too. They would spend days sitting in the sun beside their horses. Time was nothing to them. And they would think of ways to breach that fortress only because it was such a challenge to them. Boone's forehead was oil-slick and the warm lateness wasn't what added the sheen to his upper lip.

It was all right to push your horse into a shiny sweat, but no man of the frontier pushed him beyond the second breath. That was the reserve that might save a life; the extra surge of power that was never drawn upon under any circumstances unless needed at the last extreme.

Boone fretted with the delay but there was nothing he could do about it so he rode his horse to the limit but never beyond it. Parker Ellis behind him, showed

impatience too, but also a little disapproval. Whatever happened, had happened
by now, and hurry wouldn't change much.

They rode into the yard with the darkness mantling the land. The long shadows
gathered unto themselves a certain depth
and solidness, and a deep, deep silence lay
over everything.

Boone swung down and so did Parker,
but the elder man had caught the smell,
thick and head-on. He took Boone's reins
and un-shipped his saddle-booted carbine
and stood looking behind them and all
around, the hair at the base of his skull
standing straight out. Never leaving the
horses at all, he just stood there as a sort
of rearguard for the younger man who
went forward oblivious to everything but
the wreckage he stepped over in his half-
hurrying, half-fearful approach to the gaping doorway that now was a stygian hole
leading into the house beyond.

Parker Ellis knew they hadn't been gone
long. He also knew they had been there for
a long time. Maybe the fight had lasted for
hours. The Indian smell was still strong.
He was sweating unconsciously in his vigil,
standing alone with his carbine, listening
for whatever was out there in the descend-
ing night.

Boone had to feel his way. He knew the two big rooms well enough, but now there was litter underfoot. The cordite stink was strong and there was even a sour overlay of rank fear, still in there. He pinched up his eyes against the deep darkness and felt his way along with fingers and feet. He found a candle alongside the overturned table but feared to light it. He called softly to Jane. There was no answer nor did he really expect one.

While trying to piece out what had happened, he heard a night-bird trilling outside and turned his head to listen. It came again, and that time he went through the rubble and back out into the darkness. It was all there in his memory anyway. Just how the table lay on its side; how clothing was cast wildly about and the flour barrel overturned and tracked over the wadded-up hooked rugs Jane had made. It was as clear as day inside his head. He walked back to the horses but they weren't there. He made a night-bird sound and got a response from over by the smoke-house. Squatting, he saw the silhouette of their horses and went over. Parker moved in beside him and he followed the older man's bent look and saw Tyre Barlow. He was sprawled and hairless, his sightless

65

eyes run full of the blood from his naked skull. Seven stubby shafts poked out of his carcass.

"Packed 'em with him all the way over here. That bullet finished him. Them arrers was in him already. That means they must've caught him outside or got him to come outside. Either one would've been easy for 'em, the way he felt." Parker's thin, bony shoulders rose and fell resignedly. "Well — you find her?"

"She's not in there."

Parker turned and looked at Boone, his brow knitted, deepening the hairline wrinkles that fanned out in every direction from around his eyes. "She isn't?" he said, surprised. "Well — she ain't out here. I looked all over. 'Been piecin' it together before it got too dark."

"What'd you come up with?"

Parker jutted his chin westward. "They went slow when they left. 'Course there wasn't no reason to hurry anyhow, but I figure they had wounded with 'em. Pretty big party. Maybe twenty or so of 'em. I'd just guess they was Brulé, Dakotas. Maybe Minniconjous and Oglalas in with 'em. Anyway — they headed west, an' they been gone three, maybe four hours. Too long now, and it's too dark." Out of sympathy more than because he thought it feasible or wise to track the raiders, he added: "We could trail 'em easy enough, come a little light. No moon tonight, but come dawn — maybe."

"No," Boone said. There was a sickening anguish twisted up into a knot in his chest when he said it. "All we'd get would be an arrow. Let's go back."

Parker looked at him owlishly, wondering whether to speak or not and decided against it. He handed over the reins but made no move to mount. "How about Tyre?"

Without a word Boone swung down again, dropped his reins and went to work. It took them two laborious hours but they got the dead man buried in the flinty, begrudging soil of his claim. They started back through the night, neither speaking.

Boone went over it very methodically in his mind. There were no guns left behind, of course. There had been no blood in the house at all. The Dakotas had burst in then, after the fight, and that was strange for the Barlows' habits and instincts would have driven them to fort up at the first sign of danger. Tyre, of course, had fought as long as he'd had consciousness and the strength, but Jane. . . . Was she a prisoner?

67

A captive of an *akicita* band of marauders? She had to be if she wasn't lying back there. If that were so, then she was either dead or struck down in rage. The only hope lay in the fact that she may have been protected by some friend, or relative of some friend, she and Tyre had among the Dakotas. It wasn't impossible, but it wasn't much to hope for either, for the smell of blood was in their nostrils and the rampant kill-lust was a red flame in their heads and minds. Like Parker had said — friendship wasn't much under the circumstances.

"Boone — over there to the right. See 'em? Over by them sage clumps. Riders!"

Boone reined up and flung off his thoughts in a twinkling. He sat motionless while he watched them moving south and east across their path. Eleven of them. Boone swung down and knelt to skyline them. They were Indians all right. He turned, took a little pigging-string from his saddle, pulled his horse's hind hocks tight together with it, hobbled his front legs and pushed. Parker was doing the same thing. The horses went down with soft grunts of disapproval but no one could skyline them now. The men lay prone, watching. It was a prickly long moment until the bronkos were out of sight, and longer before they let the animals up and rode on, holding to their original course. Boone only half permitted the fears to grip him after that. He, like his pardner, never relaxed vigil until they were back before the big gate of the fort awaiting the new day. The Army wouldn't open those gates, come hell or high water, until daylight.

Once inside, Boone told the officer, Fleming, what they had seen. Not just the story of all the raiding parties harassing the countryside outside the fort, but the wreckage of the Barlow ranch and how Tyre Barlow had died as well.

Fleming looked at his hands on the table in front of him and spoke the only words he could speak. "There'll be a lot of that, Helm. There's nothing we can do at all. Nothing. We've sent for reinforcements but they won't get here for a while. There's a pretty strong column moving in under General Harney. Right now we're lucky to be alive. I don't know why they haven't attacked the fort, but I'm damned glad for that." Then the officer looked up out of haunted, weary eyes. "You'd better stay inside too, for the time being."

They did, both Boone and Parker, not because they wanted to but because they couldn't do otherwise. Ride out after the raiders? In the first place they wouldn't have found them. In the second place, if they had found them, they would have been killed on sight. No amount of talk, of sign language or signals would have saved any white man in the Dakota territory after the so-called "Grattan Massacre."

So Boone raged inwardly, his mind in a ferment of imaginings that wakened him at night until he was on the verge of going out no matter what would happen. When Crow scouts brought in the word that the relief column was nearing, the strain lessened a little and there was wild rejoicing.

But the days had gone by and the months as well, and gruesome stories filled the fort. Tales told badly because no one could embellish them anyway. Stories of atrocities so terrible they were nearly unbelievable, and the same old tales resurrected, that re-set the impression among the whites at Laramie that Indians were all savages and fiends. Unsuspecting people were shot in the back and killed. Boone and Parker and a rare few others who understood why this was, tried to explain it.

"To an Indian, an enemy is an enemy," Boone told a new soldier on the post.

"They kill him any way they can. They see absolutely nothing cowardly about shooting him in the back or killing him by stealth. They are sworn to kill an enemy only — count a coup on him — not necessarily take useless risks to do it."

"Awright," the soldier replied, "then why do they make those charges like they do. One crazy In'yun against a company of riflemen?"

"Two reasons. They're resigned to getting killed, or they want to show their valour. But that doesn't mean anything; only that they are showing off. They believe just like we do that a man who can kill an enemy without any risk is a smart warrior."

"But in the back."

Boone turned away from the man. "In the back. They see nothing wrong about it. That's where whites get the idea they're cowards and won't fight face to face. That's also just one reason why the whites under-rate Indians. You'll find out whether they're cowards or not — if you live long enough."

The reinforcements made it possible for a modicum of commerce to roll over the road again. The risk was still there, hanging over every emigrant's head just as it always had, but the marauders didn't dare act too boldly now. Moreover, the pilgrims adopted a leaf from the page of the hard-bitten old traders and professional freighters. They went in caravan trains of as many wagons as they could muster together, and this cut down the danger from attack considerably and made it possible for horsemen to go abroad once more.

Among the first to go were Boone Helm and Parker Ellis who rode west into the setting sun. The first Indian encampment they found without much difficulty for not all the Sioux were considered hostile. Those that weren't would become so in time because an Indian was an Indian to almost every white man and was fired upon, driven off, massacred and stolen blind. There was no differentiation made until there was none needed. But that hadn't happened yet, so Boone struck Old Calves' camp on the North Platt near Mormon's Ferry, and sat in the late evening outside the worn lodge of his host and talked.

There was much to discuss. Parker said very little. He was engrossed with the preparations for the meal of boiled dog with wild onions and sage roots the women were busy with. Boone was just as hungry but there was the haunting fear that came first. He asked who had made that raid at the Barlow's place. Old Calves didn't know — or at least didn't say.

Boone considered this and didn't especially believe it, even though he understood why it must be so. There were many raiding parties out that covered the land.

"But it's not like before. Not like just after the Grattan fight," Old Calves said. "It was worse then. Now there are soldiers again. The Indian must be careful."

"But the raiders still ride," Boone said, persisting. "They still plunder and kill and count coups. The whole breadth of the land is full of it."

"Much isn't true."

"I believe that. I also believe that much is true that no one has found out yet."

Old Calves was bowed with his years. He was one of those whom the other Teton Sioux scorned — one who depended upon the annuity goods, the metal arrow tips, the iron pots, the coffee and molasses of the white man. He was a dependent and he was old, and had refused to "go out" with his people, pleading instead for peace, which he had found very satisfying in his declining years. Besides, what came of warfare but fewer mouths to feed, fewer Dakota youngsters in the camps and more burial scaffolds?

"True. Many whites lie under the leaves and the rocks. Many will never be found. Likewise, many Dakotas will never ride in to visit again. No one can know all of it. A man has only his own corner of the world."

Boone lengthened the conversation, broadening it, and led around to the fight at the Barlows again, but Old Calves was waiting for him when he brought it up, exactly as he had been before.

"I don't know. There are thousands of the people raiding. War parties are like blades of grass and leaves in the autumn. I see them, hear of them, and know nothing."

"They took a prisoner," Boone said slowly, "a white woman prisoner. She was a friend of the people. They killed her brother and we buried him."

"Your squaw?" Old Calves asked studying the ground with pondering blankness.

"No — my friend."

"Hau," the old man said softly, then lapsed back into his provoking silence again. There was nothing in his face that indicated he would speak again.

"I don't ask for the soldiers, or the

Grandfather, or even the Father of the Dakotas. I ask for myself. I want her. I will give all the horses the people want that I can get. I will close my eyes against the killers of her brother. My heart is good — my tongue is straight."

"Hau, hau." And that was all.

Parker squirmed but avoided looking at either man. There was a dull, dark stain flooding in under his parchment skin.

"I knew Conquering Bear. He would have told me."

"Conquering Bear is dead."

"I know that. I talked to him the night before the wagon guns went to his people."

Old Calves looked up from the ground. "You went to him that night? Why?"

"To tell him to pay for the old cow. To make peace quickly or there would be great trouble."

The Dakota's muddy-coloured eyes didn't move an iota. "There are young white men with old heads just as there are old Indians with old heads. Young Indians want war. Now they have it and it grows big for them and it will grow bigger. You were Conquering Bear's friend. There have been many war parties. Red Cloud's people are mighty warriors. They range far and take many prisoners." He stopped, fixed Boone with his rheumy eyes, like the unhooded stare of an old reptile, then swung his glance to Parker Ellis, who was studiously avoiding his look, and spoke again.

"Little Thunder and They-Are-Even-Afraid-Of-His-Horses are having trouble with the Brulés. They want to join the Minniconjou. There is a great war ahead. You must look fast, for the people are wild now. Red Cloud's Oglalas take prisoners, I know. . . ." And that was all Old Calves would say, then or later, so Boone and Parker ate with them and lay down in their robes and slept. Before dawn they quit the camp, saluted a lone sentinel who leaned on his lance and watched them go back toward the emigrant road (The Oregon Trail the whites were calling it now).

"Well — now what?"

Boone looked into the new day and worried. "Not among the Oglalas, Parker, that's out. We'd never help her and our topknots'd wind up on a coup-stick sure as night an' day."

"I know. What then?"

"Go back, I reckon. Winter's here. There won't be any more trains this year. We daren't go alone. We'll have to wait for spring."

And that's what they did because they had to. Waited until the spring of 1854 like all the plains did. That winter made it impossible for the Indians and the soldiers alike to do much. There were a few nondescript raids across the breadth of the land and a few sorties by the Army, but nothing happened to dispel the awful doubt that was beginning to show in Boone Helm's face, until spring, and even then there wasn't much to encourage him. Parker was growing morose and short spoken too, as he knew he would become that day in '53 when they came to the Barlow's ranch and found it plundered. So he was glad at last when Boone said they would ride out and seek information again.

It was slow progress or no progress at all, for despite Old Calves' hint, they could find no Oglalas or Brulés. By now the Army was back in the land and the "tame" Indians were becoming less and less friendly too, for they were constantly being attacked for no other reason than because they were handy and they were Indians.

So the plains writhed in a blood-froth, and smoke went straight up in the crystal air where wagon caravans were ambushed and destroyed, and, conversely where Dakota villages were surprised and levelled amid the shrieks of the dying and the chants of the fighting men. Boone rode with Parker Ellis beside him, seeking Oglalas, but not openly. He didn't want to find them in force and killing but in such a way that he could approach them in peace and stay alive for his quest after he left them. It wasn't a simple thing to do, not with the frontier ablaze with death and hatred. But the search dragged and led them nowhere except from one Dakota encampment to another until there were definite signs of hostility among the Indians. After that, they hesitated, for no one, not even a fellow Indian, was above suspicion after a while, and it wasn't possible for any man, Red or white, to travel without death lurking behind every brush clump and in every arroyo.

By then the months had dragged and it was hot again, with the grass underfoot cured and dead looking. By then too, there was a terrible "battle" that really wasn't much of a fight, as Indian battles went, but it was swollen with all the poignancy, the terrors and desolation that invariably went with the meeting of the Red men and the white men. It took place in the first week of September, 1855, while Boone Helm and Parker Ellis were riding towards the Running Water country. Neither of them had an inkling anything like it was brewing, nor did the Dakotas, from whom they got all their information after they left the white fort.

Grattan would be avenged. The government sent out soldiers in great force with wagon guns in long lines to do it. They moved along the Platt looking for hostiles. They had their flags and their bugles and their long-knives and their wagon guns like they always did, but now they had two things they had lacked before. A wily, stone-hard leader named Colonel Harney — later known among the Indians as "Squaw-Killer Harney," and another prerequisite of any force of soldiers who would be successful against the Indians — scouts — Indians or half-bloods, or white men who had lived long among the Dakotas and their allies, the Northern Cheyennes.

They moved up the Platt towards the favourite hunting-ground of the Brulés and Oglalas and Minniconjous, who were up there making meat after a wonderfully successful buffalo hunt, packing their parfleches with winter food. Red Cloud and Iron Shell and Spotted Tail rejoiced with their people, unaware of the coming of Colonel Harney, forgetting even the warnings of old Bordeaux, the trader, who had sent frantic messages to them. Prompted possibly by his Dakota wife, Bordeaux told them to either go a long way off and hide or come in and trust in the forgiveness of their Grandfather in Washington.

They would heed Bordeaux's advice, but not right then when the buffalo were plentiful. Besides, they had a lot of right on their side. The Grandfather would see that. Conquering Bear was dead. Of the plundering war parties — well, what of them? There was no way to control the soldier societies and what they did didn't reflect against the whole tribe. But it did, only the Dakotas didn't think it would. So, while they made up packs of winter food, Harney's column was swinging perilously closer.

Colonel Harney wasn't as foolish as Grattan had been. He was a colonel and had a little grey in his beard. He hadn't lived so long nor risen to such eminence among the whites by being a fool. He sent scouts far ahead. They captured or killed the Indian sentries so that word couldn't be carried to the tribesmen. Thus he came to Blue Water Camp on the 3rd of September, 1855, almost before the assembled Dakotas knew he was anywhere near, and attacked with wild and unrestrained ferocity.

The Indians had less than two hours' warning, but they made good use of it. All thought of the bulging food packs was forgotten. This was a fight for life. The squaws and children were sent away and the warriors stripped, painted and armed themselves for war. The women and children fled ahead of a great cloud of dust — and ran into a split-off of Harney's column that had anticipated such a move. Unmounted, rifles shining, holding back, they waited until the women and children were in range before they fired.

Some few souls rode headlong into the first volley and died so, but most of them turned in another direction, also finding soldiers waiting, sweaty-faced and flushed with anticipation. Back at the main encampment the warriors fought wherever they were caught. Some running to the rocks, others standing up, wide-legged, firing as long as they could stand.

The sky overhead was red and black with an impending storm. The heavens would open up and send bolts of lightning to mark the battle of the Blue Water. Guns supplied a thunder that over-rode the crashing of the elements. Little Thunder was among the first to fall. Spotted Tail had to stand by and watch his youngest daughter fall alive into the hands of the maddened soldiers. Iron Shell's wife was also taken as was his baby son.

The Dakotas couldn't stand and face the withering fire. They broke and fled, heading for some little caves among the rocks near the creeks. Many died in the water itself about the same time the caves were shelled by the wagon guns. Indian dead piled up. Some fell in groups, resisting. Others were ridden down and sabered by the cavalrymen. The bodies were there in the terrible twilight by the score; warriors in their paint, and old women, and children. It was a wild butchery. The cries of the fighting warriors were mixed with the incoherent screams of triumph from the white soldiers. Harney stood on his little rocky eminence across the way and watched, probably the only man to have an unobstructed and clear view of it all. And in the middle of the holocaust, a young squaw who had run until she dropped, doubled up in agony and gave birth to a baby boy, so, in the midst of death, life came anew, a promise kept to the Dakotas of eternal strength, although they would one day come to wonder why.

Except for the surprise and the successful surround engineered by the wily Colonel Harney, there probably wouldn't have been many prisoners, but there were. Almost a hundred of them — captives of the Dakotas and the Dakotas themselves.

The Army herded them all together, taking no time to bother with them. Indian dress was enough. Moreover the heat of battle was still upon them and the dust was thick in the air and over the perspiring faces of the captives. They were marched ahead after a hasty going over for arms. The victory march began.

The battle was over but the storm grew blacker as the remnants of the Dakotas were marched down the trail to captivity. What was left of the Sioux raced away to spread the news of the Bad Day. So it was that Boone Helm beheld black shadowy riders against a lighter night, flying over the land under the flashing tongues of lightning. He and Parker sat still until they heard singing, then Boone swung his head.

"That's in English. There must have been a battle. Either that or it's a fresh column coming down from Montana."

"Yeah. Let's see."

They rode warily, with the fleet shadows of swift riding men all around them in the night. They knew these little groups and individuals were Indians. It wasn't hard to tell, but somewhere up ahead men shouted out a ribald song in English. They went towards the sound and eventually found the smell of dust and Dakotas strong in their faces, sweeping forward like a banner of their coming in the wild night wind. Then they saw them. Captives chanted softly while walking between lines of their captors. Some staggered, as some had right to do. Iron Shell's mother-in-law's belly had been split open and she walked now with a wet hide bound tightly over the gap holding back her entrails.

"Hullo there. Who' you fellers?"

Boone rode closer and identified himself and Parker Ellis. "Was there a fight?"

"Fight?" the soldier said, his red, freckled face aglow with triumph and old sweat. "Christ-a-mighty — it was a good 'un." Then he was past. Boone reined in by the side of the captives and stared through the darkness at them. They were mostly Brulés with a smattering of Minniconjous and Oglalas, and a few Northern Cheyennes. He turned to Parker with a wide look.

"They sure caught a herd of 'em, Parker. Must have surprised a camp."

"Yeah, and it's a good thing too, or those captives of the Dakotas would've had their damned throats cut. Come on. Let's head back to the fort. We can get back long before 'em, otherwise we'll be shorted on the chow. They got prisoners to feed now."

Boone reined out of the dusty press of humanity and horseflesh and followed his pardner. He was elated too, for at long last he'd he able to talk to some Oglalas and Brulés and find out about Jane Barlow.

They made it to Laramie without meeting any more riders, but the feeling was in the air that they weren't alone under the black, swollen belly of the heavens. Harney's plodding prisoners and their victorious guards rode up. The swarm of slouching, indifferent acting Indians who were ostensibly trading there, caused a temporary diversion when they suddenly threw up their blankets and screamed so that the Army horses were thrown into brief confusion and a few animals ran off and a handful of prisoners also escaped. But all that did was make the colonel more angry. He thundered out against the Dakotas. Most people, Red and white, thought that the Indians had been very foolish. What they didn't know until a long time afterward was that those same Indians were escapees from Little Thunder's camp who had ridden hard to get to Fort Laramie ahead of the soldiers for a last taunt at them before returning to their devastated village and joining in the wailing, the gashing of flesh and the beating of ashes into their hair, with the other mourners.

Boone nor Parker Ellis were there to see the final defy thrown in the soldiers' faces, but they heard the commotion and trotted toward the gate in the adobe wall in time to hear the scorching curses of the soldiers and their officers, and see the captives knocked rudely inside before a general outbreak could occur.

The men and Indians poured through the gate. There was a lantern thoughtfully supplied by someone. Boone stood there watching the drama of the sick, dazed Dakotas streaming forward and the tiredness that replaced the looks of triumph among the soldiers. Parker Ellis, beside him in the shadows, growled in Boone's ear.

"That'll sort of equal things up I reckon, but what in hell'll the Army do with In'yun prisoners?"

Boone shrugged. "Send 'em to the forts in Florida, I suppose. That's what they say they do. I don't know. There must be close to a hundred of 'em. That's the biggest herd of captive Indians I ever saw."

"It must've been a surround. They wouldn't have been caught any other way. A surprise and a surround."

"Yeah. Look there. That one's a Crow. See his roach?"

Parker grunted. "I seen a white man among 'em back there when we first came up."

Boone was nodding. The bedlam increased as the long file wound inside. It was almost impossible to hear anything for the racket. He was turning away when a walking cavalryman, leading his horse and bringing up the rear, came along, his saber making a metallic sound that added to the soft, dragging-shuffling of so many moccasins over the packed earth. Boone looked past the man. He was keeping pace with a young Indian woman. She had her head down and her shoulders sagged. He recognizes her in the fleeting second she was under the smoky lantern as Iron Shell's wife. He'd seen her often enough to know. The soldier was trying to talk to her but she wouldn't look around at him. Parker's growl of profanity came to him. He nodded in silent agreement. There would be a lot of that now. Then he saw the white man walk under the lantern and sucked in his breath quickly, for right behind him came a tall woman with chestnut hair that shone like burnished gold in the gusty light. Boone pushed people aside and called her name.

"Jane! Jane!"

A whisker-stubbled soldier's face loomed in his vision with a look of pure astonishment. Boone felt the impact when they collided but he clawed free of the man and was in where the Indian smell was strongest, reaching for her. He saw the quick, alarmed lift of her wild glance — then recognition. She made a strange little animal sound and fell against him.

Somewhere behind them, with the ebb and flow of bronzed and white humanity, Parker Ellis had a lanky trooper by the blouse front, his eyes burning intently and his voice low and savage.

"Put it back, ye damned fool. She's white. She's his woman. He didn't even see ya."

The soldier's glare dulled and he relaxed and Parker let him go.

Chapter Three

THE DEPTH OF CONFLICT

She was too distraught to be rational for two days. Boone had held her when she fainted and only the light of a lantern convinced the soldier officer that she wasn't a Dakota. They were separated though, Jane Barlow being taken to an infirmary within the fort and Boone and Parker were brought up before a Lieutenant Vallance for questioning.

Vallance was young, rosy-cheeked, and with a nervous habit of running one fist around inside the palm of his other hand. But he was a good listener; wise enough, perhaps, not to have believed all the older men had told him of Indians. But the things he said were mimicked from the attitude adopted by all Army men; reflections of Harney's words, "We will have blood!"

"You two appear to know the Indians well enough to serve your nation. We need you. We need every frontiersman we can get. It was because of dependable scouts that the colonel was able to whip the Sioux at Blue Water. I've been asked to interrogate you both and suggest that you join up as civilian scouts."

Boone listened with the hawkish face of Parker Ellis behind his shoulder. He shook his head slowly, ruefully. "I don't think it would work, Lieutenant. We don't see things the same way."

"In what way?"

"Like this," Boone said. "The Indians are dogs to you. Well — they're savage and cruel, I won't say otherwise, but that's the way they've always been. The Army doesn't try to understand *why* they are that way. It doesn't even try to get along with them. It wants to kill them off and we don't look at it like that."

"No? How do you look at it?"

"Make peace with 'em and keep it. Give your word and keep it. Say nothing you can't do, and do nothing you can't explain to them. They don't understand you any more'n you understand them. But they say something and do it. So far your record isn't as good. This Colonel Harney says he wants blood. Well — he'll get a bellyful of it if he isn't careful. That's wrong, Lieutenant. They can fight. Know more about it than you do because they've been doing it longer. Don't fight 'em. Make peace."

Lieutenant Vallance studied the two bronzed faces a moment before he spoke. There was a vague understanding gnawing at the corners of his consciousness. "Well — will you do this? Will you sign up and do what you can toward showing us what you know of Indians? Lord knows, we're not blameless. You ought to read some of the papers back in the 'States. Some say we're too soft, some say we're butchers. How can the Army learn if no one'll volunteer to go along and show us the way? It's easy to condemn us. Will you help us as well?"

Boone considered it. "There'll have to be concessions on both sides. It'll be hard. Will the Army try to get along with the Dakotas?"

Vallance balled one fist and put it into the palm of his other hand and kneaded it. "For myself I'm willing to learn. I can't answer for the Army, but I'm sure the rankers would like to see this mess settled as badly as I would." He smiled boyishly and Boone liked him for the frankness of the expression. "I've got a new wife back East I'd like to get back to."

"All right." Boone turned a questioning glance toward Parker. A long look passed between them, then the older man nodded once, curtly. "We'll do it but we want to be able to quit any time, too. Is that all right?"

"Fine. As good as we can ask."

They signed the papers and shook hands all around. Back outside, Parker looked gloomily at the crowded parade ground with its myriad blue-black shadows and the wavering, orange-yellow light. There was a strong smell of horse sweat, and a stronger odour of Indians in the place. He wrinkled his nose a little.

"Boone — he's a boy. Harney says they want blood. I got an idea neither one of 'em will get their way altogether. Half peace, half war. It don't never work, mark me, Boone. I've seen it like this before, years back with the Crows."

"I know," Boone answered him. "I understand what you mean, but there's got to be an effort made. We can't do much — just the two of us — and anyway, we're civilians, but I look at it like this. We're experienced and they're not. We know what's wrong and we should do what we can to show them and help stop it before

92

things get too big for both sides." He frowned a little into the night. "It's a sort of duty, Parker. Maybe we won't be able to do much, but at least we owe it to both of 'em to try."

"I reckon," the other man said laconically, but his granite profile didn't soften any. "Well — at least we eat for a while."

Boone stepped down on the little plank-walk before the hutment-office. "I'm going to see Jane. You coming?"

Parker wagged his head. "Naw. I'm a fifth wheel there, boy. You tell her I want to see her up an' around, though. I'll go look to the horses." He didn't wait to hear what Boone might say because he didn't want to be over-ridden. Boone watched him walk on into the shadow-world that was the night, then turned and made his way toward the infirmary where a powerful smell of carbolic acid smote him mightily and a harassed orderly glared with a frown and passed him in.

Jane was lying fully clothed on a metal cot. Boone winced inwardly from the thinness of her; from the look of her hands swollen and grimed from hard physical labour but mostly from the blank, deeply vacant stare of her eyes, the way they looked up unblinkingly, unseeingly, at the low-domed mud ceiling.

"Jane?"

She turned and looked at him. There came a sheen of mistiness to her eyes and a fought-down quiver around her full mouth. "Boone, I'm ashamed for the way I acted — for what I did — the other night."

He smiled in vast relief and sat down on the edge of the cot, reaching up to take off his hat. "I wasn't, but you sure scared the devil out of me. Never had a woman faint in my arms before."

Her smile was weak but genuine. "You want to know what happened, Boone?"

"Only if you want to talk about it."

She spoke, but it didn't sound like anything she wanted to do. More as though it were a duty or obligation she owed him. "I haven't spoken about it to anyone. Maybe it'll be good to get it out of me. . . . They came in the late afternoon, but I'm sure they weren't out there before. All I know is that when I first saw them was when I heard Tyre cry out. He was down at the corral feeding the horses. I ran to the door. They were riding like wild men, all painted and yelling. Where they came from I don't know but they were there all of a sudden and Tyre was running toward the house. I held the door for him and when he went

94

past me I saw the arrow shaft sticking out of his back.

"It made me sick but he didn't seem to know it was there. He got his gun and told me to get mine. After that — Boone — I don't remember all of it. We fought them a long time. We never shot together. We'd rehearsed it many times. I'd re-load while he shot, then he'd re-load while I shot. But — that arrow made him faint three times. He'd come to and try to get up. I — I . . ."

"Finally you had to do it yourself and there were too many for you. I know, Jane. Parker and I read the sign."

"Yes," she said quietly, still looking at the low ceiling. "There were too many of them. The last time Tyre fainted I had to stop to re-load and that was when they hit the door with their battering ram. I couldn't re-load but one gun and fire it. That's when they came in — while I was re-loading. After that . . ."

"All right," Boone said. "Don't think about it. They took you a prisoner. You were a slave for a year. I've seen their slaves, many times. I know the rest of it." His palms were damp and chilly feeling. "Parker sent word that he wants you up and around. I do too, Jane, so don't think about it any more."

She turned toward him with the wetness gone from her glance and a hot dryness in its place. "Did you find Tyre?"

"Yes, we buried him by the corral."

"Oh. I knew, I guess."

He took one of her hands and squeezed it hard, making it hurt a little, then he smiled. "You're lucky at that. The whole country's on fire."

"I know. War parties used to come through the camp. They had scalps galore. It was sickening. They had victory dances and I learned a little of their language and understand some of it."

"Was it Oglalas that got you?"

"Yes, but they traded me to the Brulés at Blue Water and She Dog's wife took me in. Tyre and I helped her one time when she was having a baby; it wasn't coming right. There've been lots of times when I thanked God for her kindness."

"I'll remember her too, now let's talk about something else."

"The soldiers?" she asked, looking at him again and keeping her eyes on his face. "I don't want to." He could see it in the background of her eyes and understood that too. White men were no different from Dakotas in war. Some were worse for they had no rules to guide them in their butch-

96

eries. He and Parker had seen that many times. She had her vivid recollections. The shock, the stunning nausea at what she had seen white men stoop to, had left an impression that would never die out.

"No — not about the soldiers or the Indians. Parker and I've signed up to do a little scouting for Harney's army. I've an idea we'll go out pretty soon now. I want you to promise me to stay here until I come back. I'll make the arrangements, but I want you to promise me that. Will you?"

"Yes," she said gravely, with almost Indian fatalism. "I have no other place to go."

He left her with a definite sense of some strange gulf between them. It was hard to fathom, but he attributed it to her imprisonment and the terror she had survived, as well as her physical condition of near starvation. His heart was heavy when he went to find Parker Ellis, and ran into the boyish lieutenant instead.

"Helm — just the man I want to see." Boone stopped and waited. "Orders've just come down to send someone to the Dakotas and tell them to come in."

Boone flushed quickly. "Do you expect them to do it — after Blue Water? You can't butcher 'em one day and invite 'em to supper the next."

Vallance's eyes flickered at the sharpness in the scout's words. He was both surprised and a little annoyed too. "Couldn't you and Ellis go talk to them? It's the Colonel's orders." His look was thoughtful. "Maybe that'll do some good. They've had their licks and we've had ours. Maybe it'll end there."

Boone shrugged. "We'll go, but you pass the word to your colonel not to send out any more soldiers, and to pull in the ones he's got out. Tell him to have the word passed among the 'tame' In'yuns that Parker and I're a peace commission. If you'll do that, we'll go."

Vallance nodded quick understanding. "I'll have it done right away. Right now; tonight. Will you leave tomorrow?"

"Yes."

And they did, after listening to the fort-talk and hearing that Harney had confirmed and complied with Boone's requests. It was like riding through a desert waste. There was no noise anywhere. No sounds and no people, but here and there across the torn breast of the Dakota country were cairns of piled rock and scattered bones with a little rawhide and hair hanging on them with beautiful magpies flying over them in black and white droves.

They counciled with the scattered tribesmen and found that the Dakota grapevine was functioning better than ever, for they were never molested although always watched. It took weeks because the tribes were scattered and the *akicitas* were hard to convince. In fact some of the hotter bloods refused to listen at all, but the older men were solemnly acquiescent. They saw the symbol of much death and suffering and bitter, bitter defeat, in the hurrying, scudding, dirty grey clouds that fled over the land of their people, hastening away before the frigid breath of winter came. They would come in to the white man's Fort Laramie, squatting on the plains they had owned since time out of mind, and they would talk with the Soldier-Father. But what — specifically — did he want?

Boone spoke from experience, not knowledge. "He will want punishment for those who have done the worst crimes. But there must be sadness for what has happened. There must be a purification and a final grief — then it will all be over."

"Hau."

It was so. It wasn't just, but there was no

other way. There was the sign-symbol in the sky and there were the endless outlines along the white man's road of soldier tracks. Like the leaves in autumn — too many to count on a notched stick. The Dakotas had sacrificed much and would have to sacrifice more. They would do it to remain alive. If there was an explanation at all, it had to be the one the people said among themselves, and it was the bitterest thing they had ever had to face. God no longer cared about his Red children. He had turned away from them in scorn and was smiling instead upon his white children. If this wasn't so — then why were the white men so many? Why did they have so many superior weapons? Such endless lines of soldiers? So many guns and men and turn-coat Indian allies to help against the Dakotas and the Northern Cheyennes?

There was no answer that Boone could make them understand. There was no answer that he and Parker Ellis understood thoroughly themselves. The words Manifest Destiny were unknown. It was simply that it was so — and thus the Dakotas came in with ashes in their hair and their heads bowed. It was hard, terribly hard for a proud and mighty race. The old chiefs, with their scarred chests from the sun-dance ceremonies, their proud lance stands and laden coup sticks, held turkey-feather fans between their own faces and the faces of Boone and Parker. For, while they knew what they must do, they sym-bolised their anguish at having to do it and wanted the white-men faces hidden from their own in this hour of agony.

Boone felt the pathos of it. Parker Ellis seemed to grow more and more within himself until his eyes were dark with a brooding rebellion. It was like that when they rode among the camps and made their talk, and rode on back toward Fort Laramie, accompanying one group of hos-tiles who were coming in.

Spotted Tail, with his genial, flat face and puffy eyes, Iron Chin with his soldier dignity, Red Leaf, blood kin to the fighting Oglala, and Red Cloud, rode through the Brulé encampment not far from the fort. Boone and Parker understood the signifi-cance, but not all of the words, as the walking horses went by and the chieftains chanted. They would go in and give them-selves to the Soldier-Father for the crimes of their people.

The Dakotas squatted in stony silence and listened to their chants, then, when

Boone and Parker saddled up and struck for the fort, the martyrs went with them. The Indians stayed back — all but the women of the war-leaders, who slowly detached themselves from the silent, motionless throng and trudged along far in the rear of the little procession, heads down and eyes dull. Once, Boone glanced back and saw the three squaws and reined up his horse, saying to the Dakotas: "They must not come in. This is a bad thing." He stopped there but all of them knew what he meant. Spotted Tail turned slowly and looked down at the women. His glance was long with pride and anguish.

"It must be so," he said. "They want it this way." Then he turned and looked straight at Boone. "You will look after them when we are no more. You will take them back to the people. You have been the friend of the Dakotas."

Parker Ellis cleared his throat and spat. The sound was sharp, like the distant report of a gun. "Let's go, Boone," he said.

They went on until the fort loomed up, and ahead of them were throngs of blanket Indians watching, like statues, with glistening obsidian eyes. Nothing showed in the darkness but the flatness of their faces. The soldiers received them and

Boone swung down and held his horse behind him when Lieutenant Vallance walked up with a nervous, congratulatory smile, rolling one fist in the other hand.

"You're good men," he said. "Congratulations."

Boone nodded, but just barely. "What's going to happen to 'em?"

"The Indians? A trial. But there's one they call Iron Shell. Where is he?"

Parker stamped a foot and looked at it as though the thing were a personal enemy. He didn't raise his head when he spoke. "Be satisfied, Lieutenant. There are a lot of 'em as don't look at things like Spotted Tail and the others do. Iron Shell's your enemy. Don't ever forget it."

"You mean he's hostile?"

Parker didn't answer; Boone did. "That's up to you. Listen — you asked us to do a job and we've done it. We've put the means for peace in the Army's hand. The wisest thing Harney could do would be to make peace with the leaders who've surrendered. Give 'em hell, then let 'em go back. That's what Parker means. Iron Shell's like most of 'em. They're going to wait and see. If the new Soldier-Father's better'n the last ones have been — if he really tries to make things good, they'll go along with him. If he doesn't, you'll hear from Iron Shell and a thousand just like him. You'll hear enough of his name to make you scairt stiff."

Vallance had stopped rolling his fist and instead was clasping it tightly within the fingers of the opposing hand. His eyes were cloudy with doubt and wonder.

"Helm — you talk a little like an Indian." He was going to say more but didn't. He thought it instead. They were like the Indians in a lot of ways but he hadn't seen it or known it before. It was there in their faces. In the long glances, the quick shift of their eyes, always watching, always wary. And it was in the almost bombastic way they spoke their words — in short bursts, using gestures where a word wouldn't serve as well. Remarkable; he'd heard of white Indians.

Boone shifted his weight and glanced once, rapidly, at the unnecessary cordon of guards that were being formed around the chiefs. There was contempt in his glance before it swung back to the officer. "No — not like one. I'm talking with two tongues, Lieutenant. Parker and I know the Indians — you don't. We know the whites too. We see both sides. That's why we keep telling you to make a peace and keep it. We know what'll happen if you don't. You don't know. I hope to hell you don't have to learn it from the Dakotas."

Parker nudged Boone. He turned. The three shuffling-footed Dakota women were going by. A tall soldier called out to them. Boone shot him a hot look and swung back to the officer. "That'll cause you trouble as long as you're out here. That kind of thing. Another thing — Spotted Tail left the women in my charge. I take the responsibility seriously. If a soldier touches one of their squaws, I'll take it up for them."

Lieutenant Vallance looked troubled and he was. There was no subordination in these stalwart, strong men. Instead, there was almost defiance. He was groping with a slow knowledge that was coming to him when he answered.

"I'll make arrangements for their housing, but we're crowded here." Then he looked up quickly. "Oh — something I was supposed to tell you. Miss Barlow volunteered to serve with a field hospital wagon that went out to fetch back some influenza-sick emigrants. She said for you not to worry, she'd be back as quickly as she could make it."

It was like a blow between the eyes.

Boone's glance held to Vallance's face with a shiny intensity. "When?"

"Hard to say. Three, four days. A company of cavalry went with the surgeon's wagon. She'll be all right. I wouldn't worry."

"She asked to go? How?"

"Oh, she's made a rapid recovery. Seems that what she needed most was lots of food and something to keep her busy. We gave her both and she asked to go along on this errand."

Boone didn't say anything for a while, then he turned away with a scarcely audible, "All right. See you later."

Boone worried away the days with Parker Ellis, the silent silhouette, at his heels. They smoked and watched and listened, saying nothing to others and little between themselves until a young Dakota came to them one day with an uneasy complaint that his people were restless. The prisoners had not come back although the Army had said they'd be returned. Some were released to straggle back, but not all of the captives from the Blue Water Battle. And the people had been talking. They wanted answers from the white men to many things. Would Boone and Parker come and visit among them, for they were known to be the Indians' friends. Boone said they would and sent the warrior away, then sat back and smoked thoughtfully beside Parker Ellis.

"What'll you tell 'em?"

"What I can — of what they ask."

"It won't be official."

"I know. Parker — that's the main trouble right now. This Harney's no wiser than the others. He lets the days go by and tells them nothing except to shut up and be patient, then he turns around and keeps a lot of their people and sends others back. What the hell! You can't blame 'em."

"*I* don't blame 'em, Boone. Haven't blamed 'em for several years now. You know what I think? I think I'm ashamed of being a white man."

"No you're not," Boone said quickly. He had noticed his pardner's growing moroseness of late; his smouldering resentment and refusal to speak. "Shake it off, Park. It isn't easy for any of us who've been out here and know what the Army hasn't learned."

"Won't ever learn," Parker said harshly.

"Maybe they will and maybe they won't. All we can do is try to teach 'em."

"And if they don't want to learn — what then?"

Boone smiled slowly, a bleak, cold smile.

"Then let the Dakotas teach 'em. They will, you know."

That appeased the older man with the badly lined, weathered face and the lean, hawkish profile. He smiled around his mouth and removed the pipe long enough to make an ugly little laugh. "They sure Lord will — won't they?"

Boone got up. "Jane'll be back in a couple of days. Let's ride out and make our talk. I want to be here when she comes in."

In a better mood, Parker got up and slapped at his baggy britches with a sharp, wry look at Boone. "You set a lot o' store by her — don't you?"

Boone flushed. "She's all alone now."

"Naw, it ain't that, boy. Listen — I've been watching you two for a long time now. You couldn't do no better either. She's got a good heart. All right — let's go so's we can be back when she comes in with her brood of bellyachin' pilgrims."

It wasn't to be so. This was winter and the land lay buried under feet of white snow that magnified the heavens so that a man lying in his robes at night could look straight up where the stars seemed no more than ten feet away. And the night freeze was so hard and quick that it popped tree limbs. The sounds were sudden and loud, like a gun. It was a hard winter; one of the worst in a long time, but the Dakotas had been fortunate in that they had full parfleches and ample dried fruits and vegetables. A man could hunt, but only on snowshoes.

Boone and Parker were marooned in camp after camp while they heard the howling wind-fingers that tore at the tall lodges, clawing over the deathly white country, dipping and shrieking and pummeling the bunched-up Indian lodges and hump-backed horses who stood in whatever shelter was handy, heads low, eyelids showing white tendrils of frost, and tails tucked in against their legs. They had bark to eat and nothing else unless they found a south slope where the drifts weren't too deep, then they could paw their way to the scant, sodden old dead grass.

At Little Thunder's camp they talked longest, for the old chief had been out of much of it, with the wound that had brought him down after Blue Water. Also, his age had brought a lot of fat upon him. But Little Thunder's Brulés were mighty warriors and the terrible tale of their disaster at Blue Water had alarmed the people wherever they were. It was natural too, since it was winter and a bad one, that the people talked much among themselves around the little cooking fires, bringing out the facts of Blue Water. Roughly, a hundred had been captured of which less than half had been released in spite of promises un-kept to turn them all loose. More than another hundred were killed outright, both sexes and all ages, and many more died later of exposure and wounds and starvation. But what they talked of the most was that Little Thunder had always been a friend of the whites, and yet they had broken his band like a reed instead of hunting up the fierce and defiant Oglalas, who loved to fight all the time.

None of it made much sense, and especially Harney's march clear across the Dakota territory and back again. It was like a challenge but the people would not take up the hatchet. They even made the warrior societies — for once — behave. And now Harney was over on the Missouri miles and miles away through paths lost and choked under the deepest snows, and that was good because there would be weather-enforced peace giving the Dakotas time to marshal the facts and think about it all.

Little Thunder spoke of all these things

to Boone and Parker, then he made a wide, graceful gesture with one coppery arm. "Is this," he asked, "the way to peace? If it is, it is a new way to us, but we will learn it."

Boone softened it when he spoke and the etiquette conscious Dakotas listened without movement among them. "The Soldier-Father is new in this land. Also, he is here to fight. To appease him will not be easy, but if the Dakotas want peace they must do this. Blood is on the ground and it must be covered." Boone paused and caught Parker's glance. It was stony hard and bright. He went on again. "Now the Soldier-Father wants the Dakotas to bring in those among you who are the most guilty. He sent out the word long ago, before the snow. Have the guilty ones gone in?"

They all knew the answer as well as they knew the reason — the bad winter. Little Thunder sighed. "The trails are hidden. The land is dead and the snow and cold terrible. Does the Soldier-Father want us to suffer even to this extent?"

Boone didn't answer because he didn't know, but he saw what the Indians were thinking. That Harney was a terrible man; an implacable one. They would have to dye the snow red with their blood before he would relent.

The next man to speak was Red Calf, a proven and scarred warrior, over six-feet-four-inches tall. He wasn't a tolerant or patient man. He was a warrior and a great man in the *akicitas*. "News-walkers going among us bring stories of how the soldiers are making ammunition carriers to pull behind their horses. They tell us they are making ready for war in the spring. If this is so — where is our peace?"

Boone was stumped. He looked at Parker Ellis and found no help there, in the sunken, steady stare of the older man. "I don't know. I can't say about this because we've been away a long time. Soldiers always prepare for war in times of peace. You do it and we do it likewise. It is always so."

"Hau," Little Thunder grunted. "That is the truth, Red Calf."

But Red Calf wasn't finished. "And White Beard has our people in his iron house. Why doesn't he keep his word and return them like he said he would? Why does he need more and more Dakotas to appease his anger? Weren't the Blue Water prisoners enough? Does he want all of us in his iron house? Are we all to be slaves like those others?"

Boone heard the suspicion and anger in the fighting-man's voice but didn't let it show in his face. "I can't say any more than I have. The Dakotas have a hard path to follow. I am a white man. Parker Ellis is also white and he is your good friend. We live among the soldiers and the white people and we hear much that makes us sick inside. You haven't the only bad path to hoe."

Reproved, Red Calf sank into silence and Little Thunder spoke for the last time, in a weary voice. "All right. We will bring in our people and the Soldier-Father can say who among us he wants. Then the rest of us can come back and live in peace and mourn for these new victims. But we will do it to keep peace for we want this very much. War isn't bad, but we need time to hunt for winter food too. We can't always fight, every day and every day." It was sing-song the way he said it, almost like an Indian chant.

Boone and Parker Ellis stayed with Little Thunder's band of Brulés because the weather was too bad for travel. Boone cursed feelingly and hunkered in the guest-lodge wrapped in his robe, staring into the cooking fire. "She's back by now," he said bitterly, "and we can't even get out of this one camp, let alone go back."

Parker smiled slowly across the smoke-rope that arose straight as a lance to the smoke-hole above. "She'll understand. Vallance'll tell her." At Boone's continued look of anxiety and impatience, the older man laughed outright; not jeeringly, but understandingly and humourously. "She won't worry anyway, so sit back an' eat a little more pemmican. You'll come out in the spring like a fat old she-bear."

During that winter, though, the illogical demands of Colonel Harney did two things. They split the Dakotas into two divisions. Those who were reconciled and ready to knuckle under, and those who absolutely refused to be sent orders as though they were slaves and inferiors. Notably absent from the treaty papers, signed on the upper Missouri under Colonel Harney's aegis, were the names of the fighting Oglalas.

"Why does White Beard continue to demand more and more Dakota prisoners? What does he do with these pople? We have seen none of them come back. We are afraid and we don't trust him. He is a bloody man."

The Army of course paid no attention to

these small voices in the night, but they got a very abrupt surprise when they announced that they were going to create another road through Dakota country. The road to Fort Pierre. Permission first was required by treaty. The Indians reiterated their old complaints. In the first place, as everyone knew, the roads very soon branched out into other roads as the whites went farther and farther into the Dakota hunting grounds after game which was becoming increasingly scarce. In the second place, the other road was allowed because the white men had promised they would make no second road. And in the third place, this was Dakota land and could not be cut up and scarred with tracks. The treaties very plainly said this too.

Events moved around them of which they had no knowledge. Harney made the ridiculous and outrageous demand that every Dakota chieftain must come in and tell the white men what bad deed each and every one of his warriors had ever done, and also tell the names of the Indians who had done them. That was too much. Boone and Parker didn't know it until they felt the slight stillness wash over a lodge when they entered, or heard the talk die away before them and saw the steady, smoky stare of such men as the Brulé, Red Calf. Sensing something, but puzzled, Boone went to Little Thunder and wheedled it all out of him. It was sickening. He went back to his own lodge and told Parker. The old mountain man smoked his red-bark and listened, then he sat back and said nothing, watching their fire-smoke climb into the grey, leaden sky, through the overhead smoke-hole. What Parker Ellis thought was manifested weeks later when the sun had made the plains a marshy place and Boone held the reins to his saddled horse in his hand. Standing there dumbfounded, facing his old friend, he heard the words with a heaviness in his heart that was a tangible pain.

". . . nothing among 'em for me, Boone, it's been too long. I can't get to think like they do any more, I'm afraid. I couldn't live in their cities nor talk with 'em either. Y'see, Boone — that's how it is, so I'll stay here. Can ye understand, boy?"

Parker's hawkish features were twisted into a pleading hope for understanding. He hungered for the one man he admired above all others, to condone him in what he was doing. Turning away from the race and culture that had borne him, turning back to the near-stone-age people he had lived out the winter among, seeking solace among them because he had become more Indian than white. His heart was full of the disapproval and resentment, making him see things like this. He didn't want to be a white man any longer. The things that had transpired this past winter hadn't influenced him. That had been done over many years. But the thoughtless demands, the brutal retaliation and the harshness of his own race had filled him so full of anger against unjustness, that he renounced his own blood and stood before Boone, waiting for the other man's answer, not afraid but deeply moved and wanting, so terribly, for Boone at least to say he understood.

"Park — I don't know what to say."

"Can't ye see their side of it, boy? My side of it?"

"Yes, of course. Like you can. But you can't help them here and you can help them at Laramie or this new fort Harney's built on the Missouri."

"No, I've thought it all out, Boone. A lot of trouble has come from bad interpreters and men who hate 'em for one reason or another. Indians are suspicious of all Army interpreters — and with good reason. Well

— I'll be their voice for 'em. I can think both ways. I can do 'em more good this way."

Boone saw the earnestness in Parker's face. The strong, tight look around the eyes was as though he were pleading for his life. He didn't know what to say, so he said nothing for a long while. He turned slowly and mounted his horse, reached down and offered his hand. The older man took it in a cold grip and held it hard. Holding it, he said a lot of things that came out of his heart, then he released it and spun on his heel and went back toward the guest lodge. Boone watched him go and saw the erect, blank-faced and black-eyed woman who stood discreetly beside the flap-hole, waiting. His mind went back to the nights he'd sat brooding over his separation from Jane Barlow, finally dropping back rolled up in his buffalo-skin bedroll, completely forgetting that Parker Ellis hadn't been in the lodge at all.

His mind was too occupied to notice the grey overcast or the slipperiness of the plains underfoot. He reined around and pointed his horse toward old Fort Laramie and rode with his head hanging low on his chest. The Dakotas had to sacrifice. Boone Helm was sacrificing. Only the Army

didn't seem to have to sacrifice. He understood all right, why Parker had done it,
only he couldn't shake off the feeling of
disaster — of infinite sadness — that rode
with him homeward.

Chapter Four

FOR THREE
STOLEN HORSES

Boone rode back slowly. He had been gone
a long time. He saw hundreds of strange
faces and found it hard to get used to seeing
men with beards again. Even the soldiers he
had come to recognise and to know, were
scattered, with others in their places. Lieutenant Vallance was at the new fort with
Harney, and Boone had trouble finding an
officer to talk to. When he did, it was a
great, fat, dark-skinned man with a fierce-
foolish beard and steely eyes that wavered
constantly while he listened. Then, when
Boone was finished, the captain leaned
across the table and smiled. It made his
teeth, which were large and very even, appear the whiter by contrast with his facial
hair.

"Helm — we're glad you got back all
right. I'll send in a pay voucher for you and

take up the matter of future duties with the new commanding officer." He stood up and offered his hand. Boone took it and felt the pressure increasing and used his own strength to offset it. "Come see me in a day or two."

He went to the infirmary, almost afraid to enter, and faced another new soldier who was an orderly of some kind. He asked for Jane Barlow.

"Yeah, only she's down at her hutment, I reckon. Last one against the north wall."

He went there, walking slowly and looking at the arrogant strength of the garrison and thinking back to when it had been a place with twenty odd soldiers huddling behind its adobe ramparts, afraid to open the gate in the evening and let two men ride out. It was vastly different now. Men called out and laughed, strolled and gambled and smoked and there wasn't an Indian in sight anywhere. Then he was at the little hutment, his fist raised, when the door opened and Jane was standing there with all the colour gone out of her face and her deep blue eyes staring in stunned disbelief at him.

"Jane." She looked better than he'd ever seen her look. Better even than when she'd been in the fort-house with her brother.

Fuller, somehow, handsomer, very beautiful with her thick auburn-coloured hair and her classical features.

"Boone! I watched you — I saw you coming across the parade. I didn't believe it, Boone. I . . ." She stopped, bit her lip and rocked her head over to one side a little in that mannerism he remembered so well. "Come in. I'm sorry — please. . . ."

He entered and caught all the strange, discomforting smells of the place and watched the colour mantle in under her creamy flesh and made a bold, wild resolution. He was in love with her. Always had been. Ever since he'd first spoken of her to Parker so long ago. He'd tell her — ask her. . . .

"Where's Parker?"

The question slammed into his chest like a fist. He dumped his hat on the floor and told her without really seeing her at all. She looked at him with a frozen expression of incredulity and let the silence fall heavily and awkwardly between them. It was while they were sitting there, so terribly uncomfortable, that the knuckles rolled over the door in an imperative, possessive way. Boone started where he sat but Jane got up easily, her colour returning in a frantic, frightened rush, and went over to swing the panel inward.

Boone was standing. He saw the warm, intimate smile leap into the big officer's face and his heart stood still. The man's glance went over her shoulder, saw Boone, and sobered. He heard Jane introducing them, felt his hand being pumped, then he was moving between them, holding his hat tight in his brown fist and crossing the threshold. Jane was saying something to him, tugging with insistent motion at his sleeve until he stopped and looked down into her face.

"Boone — what's the matter? Are you all right? Please — don't go, Boone."

He reached down and unlocked her fingers and went anyway. He had been away a long time. He needed a place to sit down — to lie down maybe — and think like he had in the long, drum-roll years that had been before. To talk to Parker Ellis — only now it would be a silent soliloquy — and reason things out. The officer had had too much smile. It was all there in his eyes before he saw Boone Helm.

He slept near his horse under the brittle moon and watched the star-shadows playing in the old Indian tapestry of Heaven that had little moth-holes in it from hanging up there so long, and through which showed the eternal blaze and splendour of *Odi Maka Contenaste,* the Happy Hunting Ground. He closed his eyes as tightly as he could and forced the fumes of Dakota legends out of his mind. He sweated with effort, and groaned once, then again, and finally fell asleep.

He went back among the Indians like a missionary — and also as though he was running from something — his own hurt; an unfathomable pain he couldn't out-run or close his eyes against, try as he might.

Months later, after he had been among the Indians and found them growing more surly, more hungry and restless and angrily bewildered and puzzled, the Army announced that Red Leaf and Spotted Tail were coming back from Fort Leavenworth and were to be returned to their people. He found Parker Ellis among the Little Thunders and told him all he knew, and received this other news back, which startled and astonished him. But it was good. Both were sorry that Long Chin had killed himself in shame while at Leavenworth, but the sweet was better than the bitter. Then they went to Parker's lodge where Boone met his Dakota wife and spent two days with them before he reported back to the black-bearded officer with the wavering eyes, named Porter.

"Man — I'm glad you're back. Listen, Boone, there's another assignment for you. Colonel Harney's making up a treaty and he wants all the Dakota spokesmen to come up to the new fort and make a council. Is that the right word — council?" The white teeth flashed amidst the midnight-black beard. "I'm learning, eh? Well — can you spread the word?"

"I reckon. It won't take long to get 'em to send out runners over that. Still — it's just another treaty. Suppose Spotted Tail and Red Leaf were to be handy up there. Sort of give a little talk to their people about what they've seen of the white men, back in the States. That would help a lot."

Captain Porter nodded quickly, his eyes flickering. "That's the plan, in a nutshell. Pass the word around, will you?"

"Yeah."

Boone did. It was reacted to, differently. Most of the Indians listened apathetically and without much hope, but the older ones, the ones who wanted peace so desperately and who were called Loud-Mouths-Who-Loaf-Around-The-Forts by the scorning warrior societies, were more hopeful. Pathetically hopeful.

Boone rode to the Missouri with some sceptical Oglalas and was greatly surprised to hear what Colonel Harney had to say. This was a good peace after all. It was simple, honest and blunt, and it had teeth. None of the Dakotas doubted Harney when he said he would enforce peace. They had come to know him well enough. Not long before he had found a camp along the hunting routes and, when the warriors had ridden out threateningly, he had pitched into them and fought them to a standstill, then breached their encampment and scattered Dakotas like leaves before a hurricane. Yes, they knew White Beard, and they liked what he said now because they knew he meant every word of it. . . . Peace on the Plains for as long as the grass shall grow. . . .

Boone rode back down to Laramie. There was a peace of sorts in his heart, but he felt old. Older than Ice, the Cheyenne medicine man, older than Red Cloud's councillors, older than Parker Ellis who had drawn many a startled glance from the white soldiers and civilians when he sat apart with the Brulés, dressed as one of them. He was a strong spokesman for them.

"What the devil! Isn't that a white man

over there? That old cuss with the lined face and sunken eyes?" asked Captain Porter.

Boone answered him quietly, knowing Porter would not understand about Parker Ellis. "Yeah, he's white. That's Parker Ellis. He's an Indian now."

Porter had smothered the strange sound he'd made behind his hand, and Boone had turned away from him.

But . . . that was all past. There was peace now. He believed it just as the distrustful and begrudging Dakotas did, as the fierce and sceptical Oglalas did and the prayerful Brulés and the smattering of Northern Cheyennes who were at the council. A good, solid core of peace they could build a new Plains world around.

He went back to Laramie with that thought uppermost in his mind, but somehow the word had gone ahead of him, probably with the party of Captain Porter who had come straight back while Boone had smoked a day with Parker Ellis. When he swung in the rarely-closed gates, a woman with flaming chestnut hair was waiting, and called out to him in a soft voice. He stopped and sat there looking down from his saddle at her. It was like taking an arrow shaft that's deep in the body and twisting it with both hands.

"Boone. Please — get down and let me talk to you."

He got down and stood just inside the gate, holding his reins in both fists, waiting. She was flushed as red as windburn and had trouble making her glance stay up to his own, but she did it.

"Boone — I don't know how to say it. To begin it."

"What is it?" he asked, wanting to help her some way, a little.

"Let me try it my way." She halted, looked past his broad shoulder, and spoke mechanically, with no inflection at all. "Lieutenant Reilly — the officer who came up that night you got back — last winter — spring, I mean — he is nothing to me, Boone. Nothing at all."

Once the words started, they came like an avalanche. Rolling and tumbling over each other in their eagerness to be heard. She was a dusky, dark red in the face and held herself primly erect, but it was a great effort, for he was staring at her without a muscle moving to change his expression.

"I wanted you to know that, Boone, in case that was why you left — like you did — that night. Do you understand?"

He settled his weight on one leg and let

the reins slide through sweating fingers a little way. "I didn't know, Jane. I was gone a long time."

"You've always been gone a long time, Boone. Whenever I wanted you — you were gone." She wrinkled her nose a little and canted her head. "No, not always. You were there by the cot that time. I'll always remember you that way, Boone. It's hard for a man who's lived like you to have to be kind and gentle — but you were, that time — and it meant a lot to me. It still means a lot to me."

"You talk like you're going away. Are you, Jane?"

She hesitated before she answered. "I have no one here any more. There isn't much a single woman can do here. Back in the States a woman isn't so out of place."

He flickered a glance past her, saw Captain Porter approaching and half-frowned. "Can I come see you tonight?"

"I want you to, Boone. I've wanted you to for a long time."

"I'll be over right after sundown. Excuse me — there's a man coming. I think he wants to talk to me."

She smiled at him for the first time in over a year. It was a barbed thing that went in under his skin and hung up there with a

129

little pain that made him gasp under his breath, because his heart lurched in its dark prison, and made his breath come up short. Then she walked away and the approaching captain's eyes followed her even though his steps brought him solidly, square-footed, up to Boone Helm.

"She's a wonderful woman. I didn't know you knew her."

Boone didn't speak. Just stood there waiting and captain Porter flushed a little with his eyes wavering more than ever. "Are you satisfied with that peace treaty?"

"Yes, but it's more important that the Dakotas are satisfied."

"That's right. But I wanted your reaction. You know, you're a hard man to understand, Boone. In a lot of ways you're like an Indian yourself. You've been around 'em so long, I suppose. Well — that isn't what I came over here to say." He flashed Boone a fixed look with his eyes and made them stay on the scout's face with visible effort. "I've got good news for you. You're to be added as part of the permanent personnel of the fort with the pay of a lieutenant — although you'll remain a civilian — and be housed here. How's that strike you?"

It was good. More than Boone ever

expected. He smiled slowly almost as though he were unused to the effort. "It suits me fine. Do I get quarters and horse allowance too?"

"You do. And I'm the only one you're to take orders from."

"All right, I accept it." He held out his hand. The bearded captain shook it manfully and turned toward some other officers nearby as Boone Helm led his horse towards the animal sheds with a soft singing in his heart that hadn't ever been there before.

He went to Jane Barlow's hutment after the evening gun had been fired and the smells of the place were something he'd remember a long time. Jane was flushed and excited looking. She had a table laid for two with buffalo-tallow candles and hump roast. He ate until the seams of his gut felt strained to bursting. It made him think of all the scornful jokes the Dakotas told of the Gros Ventres — the Big Bellies — who came to visit and stuffed themselves for weeks on end until their host's food supplies were depleted, then moved on to visit others. He leaned far back over the coffee and looked across at her. She was all a man might ever want. All, and it was a huge word with a great significance the way he meant it to himself.

"Tell me about the peace, Boone. Is it as good as the soldiers seem to think?"

"Yes, it's as good. It's the best peace they've ever made. All they have to do is keep their side of it and the Indians will take care of their end. To me, it's like lifting a stone off an old man's shoulders. I'm tired of riding all over the plains. Sick of talking and never knowing if my words mean anything, or if Harney or someone else has reversed their stand while I'm saying the things they used to mean."

"I'm glad."

"I am too," he said, "and I'm glad you are here and — well." It was lame. So lame he flushed and tightened his grip on the coffee cup. "Jane — I'm on the regimental books with the pay of an officer. It's permanent." He licked his mouth hurriedly. She had a way of looking at him that made the back of his mind feel naked. That made it no easier to say things.

"I'm very glad for you, Boone." It was a soft-mellow way of speaking that showed she really meant it.

"Thank you — only — Jane, I want to marry you. Will you do it? Will you marry me, I mean?"

He felt like he'd just run top speed up a

132

high hill. It took effort to hide the way his breath was pumping past his compressed nostrils, the way his heart was churning inside him, raggedly.

"Boone." She didn't look shocked like he'd thought she would, nor especially sad like he'd romantically imagined a woman must look at a time like that. Her glance was as steady as it always was, but her mouth was open a little and the candle light shone off her small teeth. "I'll marry you — yes — but do you love me?"

He felt the dampness behind his shirt-front where he was perspiring and made a crooked, very self-conscious smile at her. "I'm not too good at this. I should have said that first. Only — well — I was scairt."

"Scared?" she said with humour to match his own.

"Scared. Frightened. Jane — I've been in love with you for a long time; years. Ever since the first time I saw you and let Tyre show me the house because I was afraid you'd see it in my face." He felt warm and good. "You know what I wanted worst, of all the things, while Parker and I were among the Dakotas? To get back to you. It was enough to make a man miss eating. That's love, I'm sure. I was all primed to ask you to marry me that night the officer came and knocked at the door."

"I know," she said softly. "That's why I tried so hard to get you to come back. It isn't all one-sided, Boone. Someday I'll tell you about it. A woman suffers in silence; especially a woman who's alone."

"You're not alone."

"That's another thing. I never knew when I would be. It was like torture — like the captivity was — knowing you were out among those Indians somewhere. Never knowing — always wondering — if you'd come back. I'll tell you about that too." She was tall, graceful and handsome when she got up and went for the coffee pot on the black-iron wood-stove, walked around the table, bent and poured him a cup and caught the hungry look in his face and burned a brick-red. "And — you're the first man that's gotten a bride, I'll bet, who hasn't ever kissed her."

He reached out and pulled her down to him, felt the fullness and warmth of her mouth over his and kissed her. He kissed her twice before she pulled free, scarlet-faced. Neither of them looked at the other until the coffee cups were empty again. Then Jane Barlow leaned back and smiled mistily at him.

"Boone — I'm afraid. It's too good.

Something'll happen and I'm afraid."

He laughed. It was a suppressed sound, not unmusical, then he shook his head. "I don't think so. I hope not. Anyway — I can face anything now."

"When — will we be married?"

"You say."

She set her head a little on one side, looking over at him. "Would tomorrow be too late, Mister Helm?"

It came back to him; the way to be young which he had all but forgotten, so he shoved back the chair and stood up and grinned boyishly at her, his strong legs spread wide and his powerful arms akimbo. "No, tomorrow'd be fine — providin' we can't find a man of The Word around this place tonight."

Her eyes were wet but she arose too, made a motion over the table and teased him. "Well — we should clean up this mess."

"All right. The Indians taught me one thing. Patience."

They washed the dishes in a metal pan and put them away, then they went out into the cool night, in the time of the Moon-Calves-Growing-Black, Boone Helm with his thick hair tumbling before the onslaught of little wind streamers, and

Jane Barlow with her shawl drawn close, searching for a chaplain who would marry them. It was all done swiftly, then they were back outside again and neither wanted to break the magic of the great, brooding night, so they walked together, shoulder and hip and hand touching, and talked.

He told her of things that had happened long ago, and she told him all the things that were full in her heart. Of the captivity, of the terrified waits she'd had, while he was out, and of her love and when she'd first felt it stirring within her, and they completely encircled the compound then went back to the little hutment and sat before the old black fireplace — timid lovers, frightened, uneasy, and ecstatic.

But the terrible news that was to come didn't strike before they had found the easy intimacy that came with their love; an immense thing that grew and prospered beyond their wildest imaginings, so that life was something neither had ever sus-pected it could be. And Boone became, with the passing months, less and less of a white-Indian, although he still thought the same, so, when the stunning news came that the Washington officials had just about repudiated Colonel Harney's treaty, he was thunderstruck.

"They can't, darling. They can't. God Almighty — they just can't. Harney's the only commander we've ever had out here the Dakotas understand. He's hard and fierce like they are, and he's proven his words good. They can't reverse him — not now. What'll the Dakotas think? That no white man alive can keep his word? That the President whom they call their Grandfather, is undependable? It's the worst possible thing Washington can do." She watched him standing there with the colour drained from under his skin and his deep-set eyes fanatically set over her head on something so far away she couldn't begin to see it. She felt her heart beat with a restricted motion, as though it were in a constricting grip. She said nothing as Boone shrugged into his coat and crossed the room toward the door, opened it, turned suddenly and saw her shiver from the icy blast of night air, and looked at her like he always had.

"I'll be back directly, darling. We'll have a cup of coffee before bed."

Then he was gone and only the echo of what he'd said stayed with her so she moved to the stove and worried the firebox with the poker and moved the big pot over a hot hole.

Boone went to Captain Porter's office and found four very solemn looking officers standing there, awkwardly. He nodded around and looked at the black-bearded, fat officer. There were words in the shifting eyes and Boone waited.

"Well, gentlemen — I see you've heard. Washington's reversed the colonel's treaty. They don't like it. That's about all I can tell you right now. I don't know much more myself."

A tall, lance-straight lieutenant with thinning blond hair and too-wide mouth worn flat and thin, like the jaws of a beartrap, spoke. "I suppose you know about the Cheyenne troubles, Captain?"

Porter smiled his fleeting, startling smile, but it was apologetic not mirthful now. "We've heard a little, not much." It was a safe and evasive way to answer.

The lieutenant seemed to send out an aura of superiority over these Laramie soldiers. He was from up with Harney. "There are raiding parties out all the time. Possibly you have the same thing down here."

Porter's eyes steeled for a minute. He didn't like the talking-down-to he was getting. Neither did the other two Fort Laramie officers. It showed plainly enough

138

in the way they regarded Harney's lieutenant. "We've always had marauders. The
chiefs can't control the *akicitas*. It's about
like it is with the whites. The wise ones
want a good peace and the hot-heads want
to fight."

Boone looked his surprise at Captain
Porter. The officer had learned a lot since
he'd replaced Lieutenant Vallance.

Harney's man unbent a little, but not
much. "They're damned horse thieves,
those Cheyennes. This latest trouble was
over three critters they stole from emigrants. We demanded they be brought
back along with the men who stole 'em.
The Cheyenne chief, Little Wolf, said they
had only stolen three and would return
'em. The fourth animal was an Indian
horse, not an emigrant animal, and he
would not give it up." For some reason the
officer stopped there, as though there was
no use in saying more. Boone looked
around the room. The other officers were
looking at the floor, gravely, not interested
in the rest of it. He spoke and his voice was
deep, like thunder among them.

"What's the rest of it, Lieutenant?"

Harney's man turned and looked at him
very cooly. "The rest of what, Mister?"

Boone's blood beat in his throat. His

eyes grew hard and icy looking. "What else happened to the Cheyennes?"

There was a long silence between them, then the officer spoke as though he were reciting something of no interest and less importance. "We had 'em in for a council. It was the only way to arrest the horse thieves without the danger of a clash."

"And," Boone said harshly, "after you got 'em in, you tried to arrest 'em, didn't you?"

"Yes."

"And?"

"There was a fight," the lieutenant said icily. "A few were killed and a few were captured. The rest of the Cheyennes fled. They practically left their encampment behind. We got a lot of horses and trophies."

Boone's glance moved slowly over the faces in the room and stopped on Porter's pale countenance with its contrasting black beard. His heart was filled with bitterness and the words dammed up behind his clenched teeth were hot and fierce. Then he spoke. "And that's the end of the only sound peace we've ever had out here. The Army had it in its hand. You couldn't stand it, though. Now you've set the plains afire again." He cursed them, their commander and their policy makers while standing in front of Porter's little woodstove, his hands clenched behind him.

"I'll tell you why that is, too. Because In'yuns're dogs to you. Treacherous dogs. Animals that walk upright and are dangerous because they don't knuckle under to you. They can think like you can — maybe better — so you're afraid of 'em. You hate 'em, you *want* to fight 'em. You don't want peace and I don't think you ever did. Well — you've fixed things fine now — you and Washington. Indians'll never understand Washington sending a man like Harney out here; sending him to fight the Dakotas and make peace with them — then not backing up his word. They don't think like that. They won't understand it. They'll say no white man's word is good — and now they'll fight you. You've had it all your own way for a long time. Now you've started a real fire — you'll see that. Let's see you put it out!"

He turned away from them and slammed the door behind. He stood on the planking outside of Porter's office and let the cold bitterness of purple night cool out the fury in his face. Bitterly he thought of Parker Ellis. The white-Indian had been right. Boone didn't want to believe it and never had wanted to, but now he did. A white man's word wasn't worth a copper-coloured damn. He stepped off the duck-boards and strode across the parade toward his hutment, leaning into the sudden icy wind that sprang out of nowhere and hurled itself against him, clawing at the corners of his greatcoat, pulling the breath away from his face with chilling fingers.

Jane was waiting. When he came in she poured the coffee and said nothing. He shed his hat and greatcoat and dropped down at the table, barely conscious of the replenished fireplace and the wonderful peacefulness of their little home.

Her deep blue eyes stayed on his face, but she lacked his patience. "Well?"

"It's all true. Not only that but the hot-heads on both sides are re-newing the snipping. Now it's the Cheyennes the Army's after."

"Your coffee, Darling," she said softly and with no faintest hint of the fear that was mushrooming up inside her.

He drank it down in three large gulps. "The Cheyennes," he repeated. "The Army wants to whip 'em after all. They'll get a surprise. It won't be just the Cheyennes; it'll be the Dakotas and every other Indian on the Plains because the

142

white man's honour will be in the dust and they'll fight because they know they'll have to. Treaties are sacred to 'em, Jane. Without faith in the white man's word — they'll never stop fighting." He looked over at her. "First it was over one damned old hide-bound cow. Now it's three stolen horses."

But it was worse than Boone knew. The soldiers had managed to capture Wolf Fire before the Northern Cheyennes fled from the treacherous council. Then they had sent word over the Plains that the Indians were up in revolt and far south on the Platt, at Fort Kearney, where the Indians had no inkling of revolt, they rode out to do battle. The Indians saw them coming, paid slight attention, and thus the Army was able to get in close before it opened up. Those also were Cheyennes. The dead weren't many but the wounded were. Those Cheyennes also fled, leaving their horses and lodges behind and nearly all of their belongings.

News was slow in coming back to Laramie and Boone heard what he finally did come to know, from Indians he met beyond the adobe walls. He sat and smoked with old friends and felt shame that showed in his face when asked to explain this new attitude. There could be no explanation. None at all. A man kept his word. Boone and the Indians both, believed this.

Then the retaliation began. It was a series of violent attacks that filtered back softly, at first, then grew and grew in both intensity and ferocity. The adobe fort was seldom like it had been before. Boone watched the change come. He had seen Laramie become an army post. He had known it when Grattan had ridden out to notoriety and he had come back after the Bad Winter to find it choked with soldiers. They had laughed a lot and joked and gambled and drank when they could. Now soldiers were riding past the old gates on weary-legged horses again. The dust-powdered men with sunken faces had terrible looks in their eyes bccause, back beyond the last soldier, came the mules with their canvas shrouded victims, ripped up and down and hairless and brutalised beyond belief, bumping and rolling in stiff death.

He watched it all and knew that Laramie was only a part of it. The whole Plains-world was wallowing in blood. Days rarely passed without sickening tales of outrage against settlers and emigrants, ambushed soldiers — the list was endless. And through it all ran the thin line of treachery that had made it so. He never forgot it. Never would.

He was watching a detail of Army wagons come in through the gates when Captain Porter came up and stood beside him. It was the first time they had spoken since that long-ago outburst in Porter's office the night Harney's lieutenant had been there. Boone was conscious of the officer's presence but ignored it.

"They look done in," Porter said quietly.

Boone nodded reluctantly, still silent. He had that way about him, of waiting when he knew another person had something to say. He stood like a carved statue of a frontiersman, disillusioned looking, hard-eyed and wary, thoroughly capable and just a little deadly.

"Do you suppose you could find out where the war parties are, Boone? I mean — the big ones. The ones we'll have to lick if we're to end this — mess."

"I reckon. Is that the latest news? You're to fight 'em to a standstill?"

"There's no other way, I'm afraid."

Boone knew how useless recriminations would sound so he didn't say them. "There are thousands of 'em, Captain."

"We're getting more troops all the time."

That was true, too. Boone watched the soldiers line up the wagons at spaced, very orderly intervals, and take the horses loose. "It'll be a hell of a fight, Captain," he said. "I'm not sure I want a part in it."

Porter said nothing. He was staring fixedly at the wagons too. An interval passed, then he spoke gently. "I understand, Boone. I've gotten to see things a little the way you do. Not that I agree, altogether, but I can see your side of it. But Boone — there's nothing else to do, now."

That was true and Boone knew it. Had known it for some time. There couldn't be another white-man's peace that the Indians would trust. Even the Army knew this. And yet, in spite of everything, the war couldn't last forever either. One side or the other must win, and in the meantime men and women and children on both sides would go right on dying, being shot and clubbed, lanced and scalped. Boone Helm was in the position of a man who must help or hinder. On one side he had friends like Parker Ellis and his Dakotas; on the other, his race and nation. He would have to help one or the other win their war because that was the only path to peace now — through complete victory. It was acid in his soul and anguish in his mind, for he actually had no alternative than to help those he felt were the least deserving — the whites.

"I'll go see what I can find out."

"Be careful," Captain Porter said.

Boone turned and looked at him for the first time. There was a strange glint in his eyes but he didn't speak at all. Turning he struck out across the dusty parade, through the soldier groups, towards his hutment and his wife. There, he told Jane of Porter's request and saw the blood drain away from her cheeks so that her eyes stood out enormously and held him with their stare of terror. He went across to her, took her in against him and held her, and kissed her.

"Don't worry, honey. I've done this before."

"That doesn't change anything," she said in a muffled way with her coppery hair under his chin and her face pressing hard against his shoulder.

"Sure it does," he said. "I'm no pilgrim. Besides — I've got the fastest horse at Laramie. Anyway, honey — they won't bother me unless I run across raiders, an' I won't do that because — like I said — I'm no pilgrim in this."

"But not tonight. Boone, not tonight."

He gave in without saying so. "All right, but I'll hit out before it's light because I've got to. I want to be well overland and away from the fort before sunup, darling. That's best."

She got free of him and went over to the wash basin and scrubbed her face. When she turned her head was a little to one side, as though she was measuring him, challenging him. She smiled and pointed toward the cupboard. "Help me — we'll eat early and go for a walk."

They did. Only little wisps of the heaviness that was in their hearts showed now and then in the conversation lulls while they ate. Then they went out after sundown and smelled the strong, familiar, summer odours of Fort Laramie and were glad the heat was gone with the dying day. Summer days were hard to bear on the Plains for there was little shade, but summer evenings and nights were idyllic. They went to where an old tree was upthrust and supplicating below the darkening heavens. Its twisted, wind-tortured limbs bent awry from years of struggle and yet it still stood defiant against the terrible winds that scourged the land. There they sat upon the earth within a meagre circlet of untrodden grass. Jane's eyes shone with a strange, mysterious light while Boone sat with legs crossed under him. June had a robust muskiness to it that entered into them; a diaphanous wafting that wasn't faint but hard and real, like life on the frontier was real, without illusions and pettiness.

"Boone — tell me the things you think."

"Like what?"

"Your Indians." She was watching him with an especial look she kept for him alone; a proud, afraid look, a yearning look with dread behind it. She had a way that let the things behind her eyes show in her face, so that one might come to understand the strain she had lived under so long.

He understood although she hadn't been very specific. "I could tell you, Jane," he said slowly, "but the words wouldn't make you feel anything."

"Tell me anyway," she said, then, without preamble or reason, she added, "I love you, Boone."

It threw him off the track and he laughed at her, throwing his head back a little to ameliorate the quick flush of blood that darkened his face in the gloom. "Some other time. Come here."

She went willingly enough, reaching for him through the falling shadows with more than just her arms. Only once did she speak. That was when she said, "Hadn't we better go home?"

They didn't. Neither possessed the initiative. So they sat there in the cool evening until it became night and after a while they talked. He told her of his Indians, of men like Parker Ellis and old Garnier, the mountain man who had taken an Oglala wife and raised a brood of half-bloods — and who had been hacked to death a few days before because of the Indians' uncontrollable fury over what the white man had done — were doing — to them.

He told her how he felt and of the abyss between such as he and the Army. Poured out his heart in a way he'd never known he could. She listened, looking up into his face, wondering what had become of the calm, deep look, the supreme confidence she'd first seen in him — the thing that had made him attractive to her — and which was no longer there to see.

Boone Helm felt strangely at peace when they finally got up and went back. He couldn't understand it himself. It was a sense of shedding a burden, in a way, and yet it was more than that. More aptly, it was the feeling that he had no yesterdays left in him; only tomorrows.

He still felt that way when he rode out of the fort before dawn with the coolness and the tangy smells around him, leavened a little by the freshness in the air. It was good. It made his mind clear and untroubled. He looked into the future — and the dying night around him — with new vigour. A man may not like what he has to do, but he does it in his best way just the same because it will hasten an ending to unpleasantness. That's the way he rode away from Fort Laramie and Jane Helm.

With the bitterness softened, he made his way across the land through a vacuum that was more ominous than anything he had ever felt before. He knew fear as he went, but he also had confidence in his learning, and showed it by riding clear of brush clumps and the little spits of forest that loomed up now and then, and by staying to the high ridges so that he could see for miles all around him as he went. He was careful of his back-trail, more careful of that than he was of what lay ahead, for through his tracks would his presence be known and because his horse was shod, unlike Indian horses, his peril was more behind him than in front.

He went all the way to the Solomon River country without seeing but two war parties, and both times his eyes were the sharpest. He hid and watched the raiders streak by, painted and terrible; reavers of the prairies. His mouth pulled down harshly with the thoughts he had of the Army's stupidity and arrogance. Those fighting men would teach the blue-bellies a lesson. Then he had gone on, seeking a friend somewhere among the Teton Dakotas, or among the hardy, reckless white men who still dared to move like phantoms across the bloody land. Eventually he found what he wanted in Batouse Lavourier, half-blood son of Jules Lavourier, the voyageur trader whose Red River carts still went unconcernedly among the Sioux with their piles of trade goods, and maybe a little whiskey, until Jules would die under a cloud of war-arrows in another senseless blood-letting.

Batouse watched Boone ride up, his little black eyes hidden in the creases of his muddy flesh. He made a motion toward the ground and they sat with their guns in their arms, and talked.

"Hot like everything," Batouse said, as a commonplace opener. Boone agreed, saying that he couldn't recall when it had been so hot, which wasn't necessarily true, but it said, in effect, that his heart was good, that he came casually, which wasn't true either.

"You run a risk, Boone. There are men-of-war everywhere. They'll find you. I've just come from Dark's camp of the Cheyennes. They've been at the lake making medicine."

"What kind of medicine?"

"The ceremony against bullets," the 'breed wagged his head back and forth in good-natured bewilderment. "I don't understand it. They go into the water and old Ice takes up a rifle and shoots them. They stand up and laugh and the bullet falls out of their clothing. I don't know how they do this thing — do you?"

"No, I've never seen it done but Parker Ellis told me about it one time. Did you see them do it?"

"By the lake, I saw it. Standing not more than — that far — from them."

Boone nodded. It was a curious thing. He didn't believe it particularly, but he had heard of it before too, and by those who were less inclined to believe such things than he was. Parker Ellis swore he'd seen it, and Parker didn't lie. Boone looked up, shaking off the mystery. "Why did they do it?"

"They are getting ready to fight. There are hundreds and hundreds of them. Many lodges, Boone, many lodges and many fighting warriors."

"Who'll they fight? Soldiers?"

The 'breed's face went serious. It was round and greasy looking even in the shade of the trees they were under. "That's why I'm riding down here. There are soldiers coming with wagon guns. Three lines of cavalry, like blue strings, and a lot of walking soldiers behind them."

"The Cheyennes won't run away, Batouse?"

"Not this time, old friend. They've had the ceremony. They were getting ready to fight when I left." Lavourier spread out both hands, palms downwards, a little apologetically. "I never know who to fight for, so I don't fight."

Boone left the 'breed in his hidden camp among the trees shortly after that and rode northward, bearing a trifle eastward as well, until he came to the thin ribbons that were a white man's road, and here he kept his glance on the horizon, for dust-banners. After a while he saw them and lifted his horse into a long gallop and held him to it until the column was in sight. He watched the officers out front hold up their hands when they saw him coming, and the long lines stopped moving and sweltered in their own dust.

A scout came out to meet him. He nodded to the man, but rode past until he came up to the officers. He saw their blank looks and introduced himself, then he told them of the Cheyenne ceremony with a wary glance for the ridicule he figured they'd register, and didn't find any.

"We know where they are," the grizzled commanding officer told him brusquely. "But this other thing. This bullet-proofing ceremony. Well —," he seemed doubtful but he didn't say he was, "it's something new — isn't it?"

"No," Boone answered, "I've heard of it before. I've never seen it, but whether it's true or not, I'd like to make a suggestion if you're going to attack them."

"We're out here for that reason, Mister Helm."

Boone understood the bone-rattle dryness, the way the officer said it. "Then don't shoot into them at all. I don't say their ceremony works or doesn't work. All I'm saying is that if you use guns, they'll fight like madmen, believing they're immune. Right or wrong, they'll kill a lot of soldiers and get a lot of their

155

people killed too."

"Is there another way?" the officer asked, his blue eyes like sardonic agates.

"I think so. Use your swords and bayonets. Surprise 'em, don't do like they expect you to do. Charge them with steel and use your guns afterward — when they're thrown off balance and routed." He sat his horse, hands clasped over the horn, giving the officer stare for stare.

The silence was long before the officer changed expression. "Mister Helm — you've got a sound idea there. It's very good. We'll do that. It gives us the element of surprise again, which we lost as soon as they saw our dust and scouted us."

Boone swung his horse aside, fell back where the civilian scouts were, and rode with the column until they came within sight of the bluffs where the river ran, and could see the large clutch of tipis — and the waiting Northern Cheyennes. His throat was tight when the orders slammed into the hot July air and bounced back down the lines until the cavalry detached itself and rode steadily, at a jarring trot, toward the waiting Fighting Cheyennes.

The Indians were drawn up for battle in a deep rank. Boone could see how they were aligned, easily enough, because the column now swung directly toward them and only the distant rumble of the wagon guns broke the tense silence that engulfed everything. Then, like a ghost-voice from a far distance, he heard the keening, lilting chant of the Indians. Only a few, and he surmised mostly women, were making the chilling sound, but it was there in the panoply and seemed very appropriate to him. When he reined up, the Army moved past him. He sat with his hands crossed on his saddle-horn, waiting.

The soldiers a-horseback kicked up their mounts into a long lope and the three lines became one great serpent of blue cavalrymen. They stopped for a moment and the dust rolled ahead of them, low, on the ground. Then a deep voice cried out into the stillness and the cavalrymen moved out slowly, very slowly, and the Cheyennes moved too.

They came like fanatics, a lot of them all but unarmed, singing of triumphs past and now to come, smiling with spiritual satisfaction that made Boone marvel at their faith in the strange ceremony. The sweat running along his ribs wasn't occasioned altogether by the boiling sun. There was another ringing shout and the cavalrymen loosened their belt-guns, and the infantry, far behind but coming like a solid mass of blue, echoed it distantly.

The next action was fast. Boone was watching for it, knowing it was coming, but the Northern Cheyennes were dumb-founded. The white-soldier-riders were drawing their long-knives, their sabers, and far back the infantrymen were fixing their long, off-set bayonets with the three edges. A terrible cry went up from the leading officer, and the cavalrymen went forward like a flashing scythe, the sun running red off their sabers as they swung and swung, riding into the throng of stunned Indians. Riding through them and past, then re-forming and riding them down again while the infantrymen cheered and has-tened forward and a lot of the blue-bellies charged the Cheyenne encampment and shed more blood there.

For the Indians it was another Blue Water. A bad day, a terrible disaster. They broke and fled. Running for their horses if there was hope of escaping that way, but running any way at all, to escape the fates that raced after them with sweat-lathered horses and high-curling sabers dark and gorged with Indian blood. They had made no medicine against the long-knives, and were scattered, broken and defeated by the white man's strategy.

Boone watched it all and finally rode down to where the commanding officer was and reached over and touched the man's arm, nodded toward the havoc with his head and said, "Now call 'em back."

The officer looked as though his victory was suffocating him. His eyes were wide and the red in his face was darker than the sun would cause. A big vein up by his temple throbbed in quick time.

"Have your bugler call 'em back. That's enough. You've done what you came to do."

The officer didn't reply to Boone, but he turned aside and called to a lesser officer and gave the order. Boone was sitting beside the other man, almost as absorbed as he was, when the bugle stung the bedlam with a stident cry, and it was over with. Nothing Boone could say would stop the Army from burning the village. The black smoke was a funeral pyre for the dead and for those mercifully shot and bayoneted who were dying in terrible pain. He turned and went back toward the Black Hills. Now the tribes — the seven peoples of the Teton Sioux — the Dakotas — would gather, for what had happened to their friends would add to the terrible wrath that had been boiling within their hearts for a long time. That, and other things that were happening to the Dakotas every day — somewhere. He wanted to know where the tribesmen would come together, if they would, and what could be done to bring about a final battle that would stop the war and stop also, all the blood-curdling raids and retaliations that were like maggots crawling over the shattered carcass of the Plains.

Boone's thoughts weren't pleasant ones. They couldn't be under the circumstances. He wasn't in a dilemma — he *was* a dilemma. Knowing the things that had brought about the Sioux War, he had no alternative but to expedite the very things he disapproved of in order to achieve the necessary peace. And in order to do this, he must find the Dakotas and take back the information so that the soldiers could make their war. Then — whoever won — there must be peace. It was Indian logic, it was good logic — and also — it was faulty logic.

He rode overland seeing only old tracks. It was puzzling to him in a way, for no matter what the Dakotas did, there were still the hot-bloods, the *akicitas*, and nothing would hold them back from raids.

160

Still, the tracks he found weren't fresh. Then, he came across more and more iron shoe marks; the symbols of white horsemen. He went into camp mulling these things over. For some inexplicable reason the Indians were gone. The tracks of the whites weren't hard to understand at all. It was simply that, with the strange disappearance of the Indians, the whites were becoming bolder, riding out and overland with more daring than before.

He was puzzling the thing over when he came to the middle fork of a rushing, upland stream, and scouted out fresh sign of riders before he went up on to a tall hill where digger-pines were, and lay there studying the distant camp. Satisfied at last, he went back to his horse, swung up and rode openly, calling out, for it was late in the day and shadows were deceiving.

A man with a strong heart came out afoot to meet him. He was surprised to see Boone. Parker Ellis had been recognised from the hilltop. Boone swung down and grasped the white-Indian's hand with a grip that was matched by Ellis.

"Lord a'mercy, boy. What the devil's wrong with ye? Ridin' out like that. Damn — ye're a sight for sore eyes though."

161

Boone's smile stayed. "Who's in your band?"

"A few Little Thunderers. Oh — there's a red-eyed buck or two, but ye got little to worry over. Come on up. And say — we had a scout out. Ye didn't brain him, did ye?"

"No, never even saw him."

They both laughed low and dryly over that, and walked toward the lodge-less camp where Dakotas were eating, waiting with quick glances and wary looks, for Parker Ellis to return. When Boone Helm came up there was a thick silence — an abrupt chill that was like a breath of sudden dawn. Parker Ellis squatted, affecting not to notice, then spoke gruffly without looking up. He told them who Boone Helm was and repeated often, the story of their long friendship. He told the Indians that Boone was more than their friend — he was their ally.

Boone listened and writhed inwardly, thinking back to the smoke billowing over the ruin of the Northern Cheyenne encampment. It came to him that he and Parker Ellis were no longer like they had once been. He disliked himself and ate without much appetite while the Indians gradually accepted his presence —

although they directed nothing his way —
and went on talking among themselves.

Later, when the night watch had been
set and the others went down into their
robes, he and Parker Ellis sat crosslegged
by the dead fire, and talked. It was the
hardest conversation Boone ever held with
any man, Red or white.

"No lodges, Parker. You on the move?"

"Sure. We're goin' over to *Pa Sapa*.
Goin' to sit in on the big council of the
Dakotas."

Boone's sunken eyes flickered in the
dying light. "It must be a big one," he said.
"I've been noticing the tracks. There aren't
any fresh ones around any more."

"It'll be the biggest. All the people'll be
there, Boone. They're going to decide what
to do."

Boone couldn't do it like that. Parker
was telling him everything. It stuck in his
throat and made him want to get up and
turn his back, to ride away without another
word passing between them. He changed
the subject.

"Park — listen to me. You and I know
there's going to be a hell of a fight. We
tried to figure out how to stop it once and
I — at least — thought it had been stopped
when Harney made his peace over on the

Missouri. Well — it's all afire again. Harney's peace wasn't any better'n any other peace has ever been out here. Now — Parker — dammit — you've got to come back to Laramie with me!"

Ellis snorted softly and shook his head. "Not a chance, boy. I should've stayed with 'em before — years back — when I lived with the Pawnees. I look at things like they do, Boone. Don't blame me for it, boy, because — maybe — I was borned that way. Anyway — I've been like that for too long to ever change back again. Ye see? Listen, Boone. Harney made a good peace. I know and you know what ruint it. Well — they don't. They don't understand a thing like that. I like their way o' doin', Boone. It's simpler. Ye give ye'r word an' ye stick by it come hell or high water."

"But Park, there's goin' to be all hell bust loose now. You can't fight with 'em. You're white."

"White outside," Parker Ellis said shortly, "an' not specially proud of it, but red as any bronko buck inside, Boone. Ye are too, a mite. On'y ye got more white to ye." The bony shoulders rose and fell. "Well, I don't have, Boone. And I'll fight with 'em, right in among 'em."

Boone's astonishment was more pain

than amazement. "You can't, Parker. Good Lord A'mighty, man. That'd be turning on your own race."

"I'm not a white man any more, Boone. I want ye to understand me when I say that. I ain't white anywhere but outside."

Boone could feel the chasm between them like it was a visible gulf. He sat and regarded the older man's smouldering eyes, his hawkish face, his boniness and his stubbornness, in silence. When Parker Ellis spoke again, it was in a softer, quieter tone of voice.

"Boone — we've always been friends. We more'n likely always will be. But I figured you'd be the one white man who'd understand me. I've thought that ever since that winter morning a long time back when you and I shook hands an' you rode back to Laramie an' I stayed with the In'yuns."

Boone tried a last time. He was tortured by the thought of his old friend living through the holocaust that was ahead — an outcast, a renegade. "Parker, they killed old Garnier and he'd been living among 'em for years. They'll kill you — and if they don't, think what the Army'll do if it ever catches you. Or the white scouts. Anyway, Park, you couldn't kill your own kind — white soldiers."

Ellis's laugh wasn't pleasant. "You know better'n that. You've seen enough places like Blue Water. I could kill any man, no matter what colour his hide is, for things like that. You recollect that young girl we seen — that Oglala kid — scalped where it ain't right to scalp a person? Soldiers done it and you know they did. Hell, Boone, I could kill blue-bellies for things like that easier'n I could kill an Indian."

Boone realised he was facing an enemy. It would have been the same whether the man across from him in the moist, faint moonlight had been Red Calf or Iron Tail, or even the warrior, Crazy Horse, who was even then coming into fierce prominence among the people.

"Then," he said slowly, "Parker, we can't meet again. I hate what's coming, but I can't stop it so I've got to go along with it. I want to see it end quickly, Parker."

"You want war?" Ellis asked, his sunken eyes deeper looking, and more troubled than ever.

"Good God no! I don't want war and never have. But it's going to be war — and we both know that. So I want 'em to meet once and for all and have it out and make peace. That's the only way they'll ever make peace last, out here, Park. I hate it

166

just like I think you do — but it's got to be, so let's get it over with."

Parker Ellis sat in brooding silence, his buckskin, Dakota clothes hanging from his lank, lean frame like he was a man of bone and sinew, warped and dried out and nerveless.

Boone stood up. "By the way, Parker, I'm married."

The sunken eyes lifted for a surprised second, then dulled again and the older man nodded. "Sure," he said, "I knew it'd happen some day. Ye're made for each other and I'm glad, Boone, damned glad." He got up and slowly held out his hand. "So it's going to end like this. No — don't say an'thing. Maybe we'll meet again. Maybe we won't. But let's keep our tongues straight this last time, eh?"

Boone shook the bony hand and dropped it. His own palms were damp. There was a big lump in his throat. He wanted to make Parker change his mind but knew he couldn't. It was a feeling within him as though he had been sucked dry of words — emptied of them and left standing there like a statue, unable to say the things he wanted to say.

"Boone — I hate this worse'n an'thing. Believe me I do."

"Park — don't stay among 'em. You can be their friend like we've always been, but don't do it like this."

"I've done it and I've got to keep on doin' it, boy. I want to do it. Understand me, Boone."

"I do. I really do, Park. But it's a terrible mistake with a new war coming."

Parker Ellis held up his hand and turned away without another word. Boone stood like he was rooted for a moment, then went to his horse and tugged up the cincha. Unlooping the reins he toed into the stirrup, raised himself and settled into the saddle. He saw two Dakotas sitting up, heads on their hands, watching him. Somewhere out of the night he thought he heard a man say, softly in English, "Goodbye, oldtimer."

He reined around and started to ride south, then he turned and held up his hand. "S'long, pardner," he said, "thanks for everything." He had discovered all he had wanted to know and something else that he didn't want to believe. . . .

Chapter Five

THE BEGINNING OF THE END

Boone didn't go to the Black Hills after all. He didn't have to because he knew where the Dakotas were going and, knowing that much, he could reason the rest.

The Indians were going to have a great council and discuss what must be done about the whites in their country who were forever coming up the Missouri River in greater swarms. Boone would carry this information back to Laramie, then his job was done.

But the Indians were just beginning their job. Parker Ellis and his Brulés went up into the *Pa Sapa* country, like all the Dakotas did, and made their camp on the fringes of the immense village that was already there and grew each day until Ellis's Brulés weren't back on the outskirts any longer but in among the great horde of

Dakotas and Cheyennes.

The Sioux could look up and around and see their great strength. It was good. They sang brave-heart songs and laughed at their own fears. They had lost a lot of warriors and people, but they were still like the blades of grass, and that was just, because they owned this land.

They erected a large pavilion sort of council lodge and talks went on up there between the great fighting men and the wise leaders while the people visited among the hundreds upon hundreds of tipis, and ate a lot, and laughed. It was a great thing; greater than any other gathering they had ever seen before. There were all manner of ceremonies, for the Dakotas loved nothing better than solemn pageantry. There were competitions between warrior societies and great sings and abandoned dances. Among them were faces lighter than most — the breeds — and there were some with strange customs, for of the seven divisions of the Teton Sioux — the Dakota nation — there were also many times seven sub-divisions of each group, so it was that among them there were lance stands that looked foreign but not an enemy would be among them. These strangers were also of the people, and that made them swell with even greater pride. No one could ever count them all with the notched sticks. They laughed and made low signs and shouted taunts into the tree-tops against the long-knife soldiers and the firers of the wagon guns. This was the Dakota nation! This was defiance and triumph combined!

Up in the big pavilion, Lone Horn spoke, then Four Horns, then They-Are-Even-Afraid-Of-His-Horses, and all the talk was of ways to find the path of peace, if there was such a thing. But it didn't appear there could be any peace, for the best one the plains had ever had was Harney's peace, and they all knew what the Grandfather in Washington had done to that peace.

But Spotted Tail was there. He and Red Leaf. They had purged themselves of the idleness-fat of their prison at Fort Leavenworth, and Spotted Tail, the warrior — the man who had once wrenched a saber out of a cavalryman's hand and killed ten of the riding-soldiers with their own big knife — spoke too, and what he said stirred the uneasiness they had come to feel easily these last, long years.

"They are like the leaves and the stones of the earth. They are more than a hundred men could count in a hundred years. They are more in numbers than any Indians in the world. We can't whip them. We can beat them often, but we can never whip them."

But there were others, with the full weight of the Dakota race all around them, who knew invincibility from this vast strength. Those scoffed at Spotted Tail. Touch The Clouds, seven-foot tall son of Lone Horn, stood like a graven image in brass and looked down at the others. His heart sang for his people. He wanted to fight the outlanders so he refused to look at sitting Spotted Tail, and thought privately that men grew muddy in the head, and woman-cautious, once they had been sent back to the land of the whites, then returned. It never failed, and it was bad, for such men had no heart left, like Spotted Tail, for instance.

Red Cloud talked and the holy men went up on to the hills where they could be alone to seek visions and have a long smoke. While higher still, sentinels leaned on their lances and watched the distances with hooded eyes. Missing nothing and fearing nothing either, they were the feelers of this mighty conclave.

Nothing could be done quickly. The

leaders were gravely aware they were discussing the fate of their people and their race. They knew, if they would ever come together like this again, all of the people in one sacred place, there would be many an empty place among them. They ignored time, and rightly so, for this was the crowning epitome of all past gatherings. What was decided here was irrevocable and might stand forever as the cause of victory or the prelude to their vanquishment.

The days spun away into autumn and the land was so over-grazed, the horse herders had to take the many thousands of animals farther and farther out, until they weren't visible. The prodigious dust-banner told of their coming back in the late afternoon, and the earth shook with the thunder of so many unshod hooves.

When the gathering at Bear Butte broke up and the Indians streamed their separate ways, only one firm conclusion had come out of their long smokes and longer talks. They didn't want the annuity goods any longer, if it meant they must allow the whites to desecrate Dakota land, and furthermore, they wanted the white men to observe what every treaty had had in it, somewhere, for many years. *Dakota land was for the Indians and the whites must stay out!* There was much more to the Plains-world than the Dakota heartland. Let the whites go to those other places and keep their promises to the Dakotas — or else!

There it was, cast down upon the earth and agreed upon among the Sioux. Their country for themselves and the whites were not to trespass. If the white men couldn't make a lasting treaty, then the Indians would, and that was it. Keep Out!

The information Boone had brought back was electrifying. The Army listened and pondered it. In the first place, it might not be correct, but far more important — and each officer knew it in his heart — they dared not march up to Bear Butte and attack the entire Dakota nation. That was too much. Boone heard this from Captain Porter. It amused him in a grim way. He laughed.

"You sent me out to scout up the information of where you could strike them, and I got it. Now it seems your army doesn't want it after all."

The captain reddened and made a deprecatory motion with his hands. "You'll have to admit, Boone, that this is a little

174

more'n we expected. It's one thing to — to . . ."

"Finish it," said Boone. "I know what you were going to say. It's one thing to whip hell out of villages here and there, and something else again to take on the whole Sioux nation. I'll agree with that. You wanted 'em where you could carry your war to 'em. Well — there they are."

Porter showed anger for the first time since Boone had known him. "You'd like that, wouldn't you?"

Boone nodded. "I sure would, because it'd end this everlasting killing once an' for all. It'd make peace out here so's a man could take up a claim and make a home and raise a family. The way you're doing it will take years. Maybe a lifetime. Well — I can't wait, and neither can all the others who want to make their homes. I won't live forever."

"Listen, Boone. We could go out there and fight them, but we are afraid to get whipped. Do you understand? Hell, that'd put us even farther back, and then you'd never live long enough to get your claim. We've got to work it differently. Oh — I was just as sick at heart as you were over what happened to Harney's treaty. But that's not what counts. We're here to win and we've got to do it. For that reason we can't gamble or rush up there to the Black Hills and tie into 'em and risk a drubbing. Hell, they might lick us and we don't want to lose what we've already gained."

Boone understood all right, it was simply that he couldn't condone the way the Army went about it. He shrugged. "I'll be around if you want me."

Porter's fat, bearded face softened a little. "Sure," he said. "I'll see you as soon's anything worth telling comes in."

Boone went back and found Jane baking. She gave a quick squeal at the sight of him, ran head-on and threw herself into his arms. He had a second when he thought she was heavier, more solid, than when he'd left. The thought was gone in the questions she inundated him with. He answered, watching her work until she was finished, had wiped her hands on an apron and made him some coffee.

They drank it sitting together across their table in the mellow evening of near-winter with the fireplace warming them. He relaxed all over, a luxury he hadn't allowed himself in months, not since he had ridden out to find the war parties.

He told her of Parker Ellis too. It made the silence that followed more poignant between them, so that when Captain Porter came after the evening gun had been fired, they were almost glad to see him. He beamed and accepted his place at the supper table, uninvited but welcome just the same. He raved of Jane's meal, then sat back and talked into the quiet they left to him.

". . . a lot of trouble on the way. We've had reports of warrior bands north of us raising old Nick." He spoke a little longer about the errors they had made, Red men and white, then looked squarely at Boone. "What, exactly, do you think will come of this big council they've had?"

"War, Captain. They're full up to here." He indicated his throat with the edge of his hand, palm downward. "They are sick of promises, trinkets, and starvation. They're going to fight to the last straw now. I'm convinced of that."

"You're not alone in your opinion. There are a lot of others — the oldtimers — who feel the same way. All right, we'll have a war then. Now, I'll ask you what I came over to find out."

"Shoot," Boone said, catching his wife's eye and winking very solemnly at her.

"You remember that white man who was with the Brulés at the peace council?"

Boone stiffened up inside. His eyes were locked with the wavering glance of Captain Porter. "Yes, I remember him. What about it?"

"Would he come in and tell us what he knows of their warriors and plans?"

"You could drag him in behind a horse," Boone said stonily, "and you could tear his tongue out by the roots and he'd spit the blood in your face before he'd speak a word of information."

Captain Porter looked startled at the vehemence in Boone's voice. "Do you know him pretty well?"

"Very well. Well enough to know that what you've just asked is absolutely impossible."

"I see. Well — all right. It was just an idea. I hate to send you out again — now." He arose and thanked Jane for her hospitality and left. Boone went with him to the door and dropped the big bar behind the panel and leaned on it, looking across the warm room at his wife.

"What do you suppose he asked that for?"

"About Parker? Oh, because he saw him with the Indians, I suppose, and thought he'd have a lot of good information. Wouldn't that be it?"

"Maybe. I don't know."

He had all but forgotten it as the fort began to pall a little with days of inactivity, waiting for orders that never came. He had forgotten it entirely when work came down the country by way of a powerful throng of Hunkpapas and Minniconjous. They had not only stopped a soldier column, but had turned it back with express orders never to enter the Dakota country again. Then, the stories of raids and fights and isolated murders and atrocities began again, and to top it off, he heard with surprise that the Dakotas had sent an open declaration of war to their ancient enemies, the Crows, with a promise to come soon to fight them.

He was frowning in thought when Jane opened the door and let him in. "Funny thing, honey," he said. "The Dakotas have sent a challenge to the Crows and have started their hell-raising again."

"But you said that would happen, Boone."

"But not the raid against the Crows. It's almost like they're trying to close their eyes to the Army and are going back to the old ways again. It's strange."

It was strange too, but not to General Harney. When he heard of the Army column being forced out of Indian country he exploded into characteristic wrath. Meanwhile, the Hunkpapa Dakotas rode for the comparatively unmolested hunting country of the northland, where the No Bows and Minniconjous were already drying meat against the winter ahead. Four years after the killing of Conquering Bear, the Dakotas had finally become fairly well consolidated against their common enemy — the white man.

Boone watched events with a thoughtful eye, and when Harney arbitrarily appointed Bad Wound chief of all the Dakotas, and deposed Man Afraid, he smiled in the thin, saturnine way he had, because he knew Old Squaw-Killer, Harney, could no more make a Dakota chieftain than he could fly. It would also amuse the Indians, when they heard of it, and Boone could imagine the amount of ribbing Bad Wound would have to take.

He told Jane and she shook her head in a doleful way. She sat down by the fireplace with him and talked, and Boone got his greatest surprise then, for he had never taken the time, really, to understand her mind — her thoughts.

"Boone — you want this war to end, but honey, it never will." She watched the surprise come into his face and hurried on.

"Listen, and tell me if I'm wrong. I love you, Boone, and what you want for us I want also, but I've been thinking and these are the things I've come to believe. In the first place, there are too many soldiers and too many Sioux. Neither side can whip the other for a long time because both are strong and fierce. In the second place, Indians and the whites are too far apart in everything; in their beliefs, their ways of life, even their religions and logic. They can't live side by side like the peace commissioners want them to. They're entirely too scornful of each other and too altogether different." She stopped, looking earnestly at him. "Am I wrong, Boone?"

He looked into the fire for a moment before he answered. It was hard to agree with her. Very hard, because what she was saying was that the very thing he wanted to end, wouldn't end. But the things she said were true enough, too. He nodded. "Both sides are strong and different from one another, but if they don't get their war over with . . ."

"That's just it, Boone. If — they don't. That's what's making you think the way you do. You want them to so badly you're forcing things and showing contempt for the Army when it won't ride out and take the initiative in a final battle."

He looked around at her. "Well? Shouldn't I? After all, Jane, you don't want to live the rest of your life in this damned mud fort. If we have children, we don't want to raise 'em here." He saw the sudden pallor in her face and the wavering look, but paid them no attention as he went on in a deep, slow way of speaking that he used when pondering what was close to his heart.

"We want our claim and a home of our own, darling. I want that piece of prairie next to your old place. It's good land. We could prosper out there, but if the Dakotas and the Army don't get their squabbling over with, we'll never get it."

"Boone — go file on that adjoining section and get title to it. Then — when the times comes, we'll move out there. The old home is still good. Tyre built it to stand for a long time. Well — you get the land and we'll wait, but I don't think it'll be long before we can move out, honey. I really don't."

He was nonplussed. "Why don't you, Jane? Good Lord, the way this situation is now, neither side's going to budge an inch. They'll be fighting for twenty years yet."

"That's probably true enough, Boone.

Only I don't believe they'll be fighting here — not around Laramie — not out by our land."

An inkling of what she thought came to him slowly, almost reluctantly, until he opened his mind to it. Then it was clear enough but he didn't speak until he had examined the prospects carefully. He straightened in the chair and bent forward, resting his arms on his legs and staring into the fire.

"I think I see what you mean. Funny, too, because the very things that can make this happen are the things I've always disliked. The coming of the pilgrims. Hundreds and hundreds of them. Well — for every ten the Dakotas kill off, a hundred more come up the river an' over the plains with their wagons." He straightened up, twisted and looked closely at her. "I never saw that before, Jane, darned if I did. You're smart, too. Cussed emigrants, like ants, crawling in here in herds. I see what you mean, and you're right. I've been blind. Too many things have soured me. I was getting so's I hated everything. Getting barn-sour like an old horse." He got up and crossed to the fireplace, swung around with his back to it and stood on powerful legs, spread wide, gazing at her with a new light in his face.

"Sure, that's exactly what's going to happen. The Dakotas will be fighting twenty years from now — but not around here. The very numbers of the emigrants'll force 'em back, if for no other reason than because there won't be any game left for 'em to live on. They'll be pushed way back into their mountains, Jane — you're right."

He stood there with a fixed look. She sat with her hands in her lap and smiled up at him. "We'll get our ranch, Boone," she said softly. "Be patient a little longer, honey. It's coming."

He threw back his head and laughed. "Damn, you're a beautiful woman, Jane, an' a wonderful one — and a good cook — but the rest of it's more'n I deserve. You're wise, too."

She squirmed, then got up and went to the stove and poked savagely in the firebox with her back to him to hide the tears that stung their way into her eyes.

But he went to her, put both arms around her from the rear and tugged her to him. He kissed her behind the ear where the dark burnished copper of her chestnut hair was softest. She struggled against his embrace until she was facing him. Her hands went up around his neck and pulled his head down until she could cover his mouth with her own, and at that second a rumble of knuckles across the oaken door startled them both.

Boone strangled the curse and scowled. Jane laughed softly, tantalisingly, and pulled loose, crossed the room with a scarlet blush and swung the door inward. It was Captain Porter with a look so black he didn't see their preoccupation. He nodded, stepped past Jane, and looked squarely at Boone.

"I'm sorry, Boone, but could you come over to my office with me?"

Boone ignored the officer's fearful look, shot Jane a glum glance, saw her widening, wicked little smile from behind the fat captain, and shrugged disgustedly.

"I reckon." He avoided both their glances until he had his hat on the back of his head and his coat carelessly draped across his arm. He hesitated at the door, leaned down and kissed his wife and swore a mellow oath into her ear, spun away and followed Porter out across the parade with the soft ripple of her teasing laughter in his head.

His surprise was greatest when he entered Porter's office and saw the erect, bandaged body of a Dakota warrior standing between two dusty, grim-faced enlisted troopers. There were other officers there too, but he ignored them and was only conscious of them as part of the immediate background.

The warrior was Red Calf of the Brulés. Boone recognised him and remembered him well from the winter he put in with little Thunder's band. The buck recognised Boone, too, and spoke in greeting.

"How Kola."

Boone replied through his surprise and Captain Porter spoke into the stillness that followed both greetings. "He got knocked unconscious in a skirmish, Boone. Is he an Oglala? Do you know him?"

"Yes, I know him. He's Red Calf, a Brulé."

"Question him, will you? Apparently he doesn't understand English." As an afterthought, Porter added, "At least he won't speak it."

"Not many of 'em will, Captain. More understand it than you think." He nodded at the Dakota again and asked about Parker Ellis. "Where is *Wambdi Ska*, White Eagle, the Dakotas call him?"

Red Calf's face was puffy. There was a matted clot of hair and blood where he'd been wounded. "White Eagle wasn't with us. This was a raiding party of my soldier-society. White Eagle was back with the people."

"Where did you raid?"

"An emigrant train. We needed fresh horses and powder with balls. We needed coffee and sweet-lumps. We own this land and we take from those who invade it. We are strong and our hearts are strong."

Boone saw Red Calf working himself up into a lengthy oration and headed it off. "How many of the *Ozuye We' Tawatas* (men of war) were with your party?"

Red Calf made a slighting, scornful gesture using both hands. "Not many. Ten. It was only one emigrant train with no more than thirty white men with it."

Boone nodded over the implication of who were the greatest warriors. "Where was this raid?"

The Dakota threw one arm westward. "Not far from here. Maybe as far as five rifles would shoot."

Boone was startled. So close to Fort Laramie. The Indians were getting bolder. He could imagine why, after their big gathering in the Black Hills. "That was a foolish thing to do. *Kin Akicitatipi Yuha O'ta Haska We Tawata, O'Kini Unkiyepi Tawacin Yuha O'ta Nagiyeya.*" (This fort has many pale-skinned warriors, maybe you will have much trouble.)

Red Calf smiled with a savage look in his black eyes. He stared down at Boone when he answered and every man in the room, whether he understood or not, felt the Dakota's fierceness. *"Owgh, Koda* Boone — *Unkiyapi Yuha Hiya Kopipi Etanhan Kin Haska Wakansica!"*

Captain Porter interrupted. "What's he saying, Boone? I don't like the look of him."

"He said, 'Agreed, friend, Boone — but we have no fear of the pale-faced devils'."

"Did he tell you how many of them hit the emigrant train?"

"He said ten. How many'd you hear there were of them?"

Porter hesitated, glanced at a youngish looking sergeant-major, then looked back towards Boone when he spoke. "The troopers said there were at least fifty."

Boone was watching the sergeant-major's face. He saw the man's blush, understood it, and smiled wryly. "Well — sometimes they seem that many. They make a lot of noise, y'know."

"See if he'll say anything about their plans."

Boone turned back towards Red Calf.

"Why are your people raiding down here? Why aren't they up in the north country making ready for winter?"

"The buffalo are plentiful in the north country," Red Calf said. "Our people are up there hunting now. Down here there is no food any more, only plunder. The *akicita* have had an early hunt and it was good, so they came down here to raid a little. We need coffee and sweets and guns, too."

"What of your treaties with the whites?"

Red Calf's smile was slow and saturnine. "What treaties?" he asked. "There are no longer any treaties. We do not recognise them any more. They are scraps of paper and nothing else. The white man is a great liar. If he was as good a fighter, we wouldn't come down here. But he isn't."

"He can become as good a fighter as the Dakota," Boone said evenly, and as he said it an idea was forming in his mind. A man can vacillate, but when his mind is made up, he will think straight. Boone was such a man.

"No," Red Calf said disdainfully, "it isn't so. We have brave-heart songs. The white man has none. We have nothing but warriors. The white man has a special race of soldiers. All other white men are easy to kill."

Boone's colour was high from the taunting, smiling way Red Calf spoke. He remembered him as an aggressive buck in Little Thunder's camp. "Very much has happened. All right. You are a warrior and I respect you, but I say this to you and mean every word of it. If you ever come this close to Laramie again, you and all your men will be killed. Take this into your heart and bear it back to your people — to your *akicita* — for it is true and I have spoken."

Red Calf started to reply, then checked himself and blinked down at Boone. "Are you speaking the truth? I won't be put into the iron house?"

Boone turned to Captain Porter. "What're you going to do with him?"

"Lock him up and hold him, of course."

"No, let him go. Turn him loose."

Porter wasn't the only officer who looked startled. They all did. The two weary troopers glared at Boone Helm, their eyes eloquent with the words they couldn't utter. The captain swore a robust oath.

"Boone — what're you talking about? He's a warrior. Look there — that's his lance one of the boys brought in. See that yellow hair on it? Don't be ridiculous. He should be shot, really."

190

Boone waited until the tirade had died away, then he turned fully and spoke. "Listen to me. I wasn't going to say this until later — when I'd had time to thresh it out in my mind, but now I'll have to. They're raiding down here because, like Red Calf says, it's easy pickings. The emigrants are farmers, not fighters. All right, I want to show them differently. I want to get the Army's permission to enlist a company of scouts — call them what you want to — and I want to lead these men against the Dakotas. I want the Indians to be whipped so badly around the Laramie country that they'll stay up in the north country where the game is. If they're licked good and hard, they'll never come back. I know them. There's no game left for them to live on down here. Red Calf's already said that. There's only one thing draws raiding parties down this way and that's the easy plunder of the emigrants. What I'm asking is that I be allowed to meet them on their own ground and whip the hell out of them so they'll lose even their last excuse for coming down here at all." He stopped speaking and waited.

Captain Porter regarded him steadily for a while, then shifted his glance to the

191

Dakota buck. "What's he got to do with it?"

"I've taunted him, Captain. The same as dared him to come back with his warrior-society friends. If you'll let him go he'll go back and brag. That's what I want him to do. I want him to get his friends stirred up enough to ride down here and try to belittle me. Will you let him go, now?"

Porter wagged his head. "I'll have to talk to my superiors." He looked for support from the other men. They were all staring at Boone. When Porter turned back, the two vertical lines above the pinched-in bridge of his nose came together in a little, annoyed, uncertain, frown. "Come on over to the Commandant's place with me, Boone. We'll see what he says." He nodded to the others. "Stay here and watch this buck In'yun, will you?"

Porter asked questions as they crossed the parade but Boone rarely answered. The idea was still too new to him. He wanted to think it over carefully before he went up against the general. After all, it may have been born out of his talk with Jane, but until he'd seen Red Calf, it had been a vague thing, and now he was being projected into it almost before it was solid in his own mind.

They went past the orderly and into the general's office. There, Captain Porter, stiff at attention, his eyes jumping all over the room, told the Commandant of Boone's proposal. The general listened, then shot a fast glance at Boone and spoke in a rumbling voice.

"Impossible. It's too far-fetched."

Stung, Boone spoke without waiting to be addressed. "Maybe it is, but it can't be any worse than the Army's way of fighting. I'm not asking you for help, only for permission."

The slate-grey eyes were unblinking. "And where'll you get the men, Mister Helm?"

"From the scouts and emigrants. They'll fight, don't think they won't. I'll teach them to fight like the Indians."

"They haven't done so well under us, Mister Helm."

"Neither have I," Boone said bluntly, "and for the same reason. The Army doesn't fight Indians — it fights the newspaper reports back in the States, and it fights like all armies always have. Well — this is a hell of a lot different. In'yuns don't fight like white soldiers do."

"No," the general said dryly, "they certainly don't. I've been in a lot of skirmishes and I've yet to see Indians stand up and fight a pitched battle."

Boone almost swore. "In'yuns, General, think so much differently from the way we do, they can't act the same way. We take a stand on ground that's ours and fight until we're killed defending it. In'yuns don't look at their homeland like that. An acre of land means nothing to 'em. Their tipis, villages mean nothing to 'em. The land they stand on doesn't belong to them as individuals, so they won't defend it. *All* the land belongs to *all* the In'yuns. That's the way they look at it. They'll fight and retreat, fight and retreat, but they won't stand in pitched battle to repel invaders because they have more land to fall back to." Boone made a wry face. "I can't explain it too good in words. It's the way an In'yun thinks. You came into their land, you're fighting them on their own terms, in their own country, but you don't fight 'em right so you just go on skirmishing and never win much. What you win today, they sneak in and take back tomorrow."

Captain Porter was perspiring. His eyes had an uncomfortable look. He was still stiffly at attention. The general was leaning back looking at Boone. His face told nothing, but his eyes were unblinking and intense in their study of the scout. Then, he nodded his head a little.

"Go on, Mister Helm. Tell me the rest of it."

Boone did, saying what he wanted and how he wanted to train the men. When he had spoken his full, he stood there, gazing down and waiting with his heart in his throat, for the decision that was long in coming.

The general ran a hooked set of fingers through his beard. He dropped his glance from Boone's face and studied his desk for another long moment. Finally, he reached far over and flipped open the lid of a cigar box.

"Have a cigar, Mister Helm. You too, Captain. And Porter — relax will you? You look like you're about to bust a blood-vessel."

Boone took the cigar and held a match for the general's cigar, then for Captain Porter, who risked firing an appalled and uneasy look at Boone over the flare of the sulphur match. Boone ignored it blandly while lighting his own, then the commandant spoke through the fragrant smoke that greyed up the little office quickly.

"Mister Helm, it's possible you're right. Lord knows we've tried a lot of things. All right, I'll go along with you, but I believe you'd have more success with regular soldiers."

"I think differently," Boone said bluntly. "I don't want to have to spend weeks untraining soldiers. They've had spit and polish pounded into them so long they'd always be soldiers. In a pinch, they'd fight like soldiers. That's exactly what I don't want."

"Well," the general said, imperturbably, "I'm going to over-ride you in that. Not arbitrarily, Mister Helm, but because I couldn't authorise you to take civilians from the post and make another army here." The slate-grey eyes were level and uncompromising. "If you'll take soldiers, I'll give 'em to you. You can train 'em any way you want, but keep me posted. It'll be soldiers or nothing."

Boone didn't hesitate. "Then it'll be soldiers, General, and I'm obliged to you. When can I have 'em?"

The general smiled for the first time. It made creases fan out from his eyes. "Today, if you want 'em. That solve everything?"

"No. One more thing. There's a Dakota prisoner here by the name of Red Calf. I've filled him full of brag and I want him turned loose so he'll go back and tell his people what I said. That's what brought us over here in the first place. Captain Porter said he couldn't turn the buck loose without your permission."

The general looked over at Porter and raised his eyebrows. "What're your objections to Mister Helm's idea, Captain?"

"None, Sir," Porter said. "I just didn't want to act without proper authority."

"You've got the authority as of now, Captain. If you two want to turn this redskin loose — go ahead. Anything else?"

"No, Sir," Boone said and Captain Porter echoed him.

"All right. Mister Helm, I've heard of you and I've liked what I heard. Anything routine, see the Captain here. Anything bigger — come directly to me. Understood?"

"Yes, Sir."

"Then draw your men from Captain Porter and — good luck."

They left the commandant's hutment and walked back out into the sunlight. Porter drew a limp handkerchief from somewhere under his tunic and wiped his face very carefully with it. "Boone — you got away with murder. Lord! I thought he'd hit the ceiling. He's pretty bad tempered, or hadn't you heard?"

Boone was thoughtful. "I hadn't heard," he said. "Let's get over to your place and work out the details."

The captain threw him a long, deliberate look, moved his lips to himself and followed the civilian back across the parade with a thoroughly relieved look on his face.

The idea was still nebulous, right up to the time Boone had been assigned his men. They were volunteers, every one of them and he made them conscious of it with a form of training that would have been far more appropriate among a scouting company than a regular army contingent.

The days weren't long enough. Boone's enthusiasm, grim and savage in a way, wore off on his men. They became versed in hit-and-run warfare. They learned to read sign and make it deceptively, how to make an enemy fight on his own grounds and when to skip out under fire. The entire training period wasn't more than six weeks, but the men learned a lot. Along with it, they had picked up a peculiar *esprit de corps*. Boone encouraged this. In fact he encouraged every breach of military regulations they tried out, until Captain Porter groaned and the general swore. They laughed at the slouched hats, the unclean tunics and pants, and the scuffed boots, at everything, in fact, except the hard, suspicious glance that never stayed still when Boone Helm's rangers rode out for their first test.

Jane stood in the shadow of an overhang and watched them go. She shared, with the rest of the garrison, a peculiar anticipation, for what Boone hadn't told her, rumour had. The men were a tightly knit, resourceful coterie of hard-riding, straight-shooting irregulars, untrained and re-trained. Boone rode at their head with a wiry, Irish army sergeant, with a button of a nose and baby-blue eyes, as his second in command.

There was no rank to speak of; no call to show respect unless it was earned. The men were individual fighters, like their foemen were. They would fight that way.

Boone led them through the night, their first time out. He made only one stop for water and none for food. He went straight up into Dakota country and had videttes criss-cross the land for sign. He sought a fight and wanted one and went straight where he'd get one.

Under the circumstances it didn't take long to find a war party. The wispy sergeant took Boone the news from the scouts.

"Band o' Injuns about three miles nor't o' us, Boone. 'Bout thirty, the boys say."

Boone studied the land and thought aloud. This was their first test. He wanted it to go right, otherwise they would lose a lot — and their hair too. Making fast decisions when he spoke, he rode on up the game trail they were following. "Good. We've got an hour of daylight. You ride on ahead and detail two scouts to get above the hostiles an' keep 'em under study. Send the rest back to guide the column in single file. Pass the word we'll hit 'em after dark when they're bedded down. Detail three men to find their sentinel and take care of him. Send those men on ahead right now with a word to be damned careful."

The sergeant nodded and swung his horse. The blue of his eyes was shades darker. As a regular army man, he welcomed action. As a member of Helm's company of irregulars, he wanted to see how good this new-fangled training would be; this unorthodox business of fighting and running, and riding forever with one eye on the horizon, the other on the ground for "sign."

The men came to life when the sun sank lower. The scouts came back like wraiths and led the column in. Boone's pulse was running fast. He was glad for the early shadows. All through the training he'd made himself appear calm and just a mite bored. Now, he didn't want any of them to see his uncertainty and anxiety.

The men rode in absolute silence, in a serpentine line. When the scouts stopped and motioned with their arms toward a slight rib of rolling prairie ahead, every trooper understood. Over that land-swell lay the proof or the undoing of all their training. They bunched up around Boone. He perspired in the shadows and waited. The sun was half gone over the horizon. He was fuming and fighting to keep from squirming in the saddle when a single, quick flash of light came from the east a half mile or so away. He sighed audibly and nodded to the sergeant.

"That accounts for the sentinel. Every man knows what his job is. Go down the line and check with them. Make sure, Sergeant. Let's go."

They moved slowly, across the dusky world of shadowy space. Tension gripped Boone's stomach and knotted the muscles of every man who followed behind him. When the second flash of light came it used the last vestiges of daylight to blink out the signal from the top of the rolling land. Boone twisted in the saddle and held his hand far aloft, hand upright and fingers together. Silence — be careful. Then he balled up his fist and brought the arm down to his shoulder and held it there for a moment. Sit-wait. The irregulars understood.

They rode slowly forward until the scouts who had signalled from the ridge came swinging down to them. He stood in his stirrups and motioned that so far, all was well. He twisted back once more and made the dismount-sign, watched as the troopers swung down and handed their horses to the horse-guards, tugged out their carbines and started past him up the hill. They went separately, each man being trained to fight as an individual. It was hard not to feel pride in them, and Boone did.

He sat motionless, watching. Not quite one-half of his men split off and followed one scout around the east end of the rolling land. The balance went straight up until they were within ten feet of the top, then lay down and waited. It was a long wait for all of them, but for Boone it was especially long. He clenched his fists and prayed under his breath. He couldn't recall ever doing it before. Then there came a distant, very faint trilling. The cry of a night hawk was realistic enough. The men on the near side of the hill got to their knees and followed one of the scouts forward, straight up.

What came next made Boone want to voice approval. The quick, dry thunder of stampeded horses. It had worked. After that, events moved almost too swiftly for him. His earlier resolve, to test these re-made soldiers by staying completely out of their first fight, was lost in the surge of hot blood. He booted out his horse and rode up the hill in a flurry of flying earth. He was still a long way from the top when the first rattling fusilade of gunfire erupted. Then came the howls and more firing. Somewhere, over the other side of the rib, came answering cries. They were astonished, angry yells.

Boone stood in his stirrups and motioned the horse-holders forward. They were watching for the signal and came up in a wild charge, stirrup leathers flapping. They swept past him the same way.

He rode after them, spitting out dust and dry saliva, until he was on the ridge. Down below were Indians afoot, their horses gone and their retreat cut off. They were firing in relays like the troopers were doing, but the difference between Indians out in the open at the mercy of their attackers, and Boone's irregulars, prone and using every available brush and rock and segment of dirt for cover, was shown in the number of face-down Indians.

The action was swift and terrible. In a matter of minutes it was over. Seven Dakotas stood bunched up, shooting and howling their death chants under a sky turned black and ominous. Orange winks of gunfire showed how well they had been surrounded. Boone's pride was solid within him. He could feel it even in the night around him, scented with the black-powder smells. He yelled out for the men to stop firing and after the bedlam had died down, he told them to hold their surround, to fire into the ground and make the Dakotas exhaust their ammunition, so they could capture them alive.

It took most of the night, but it was accomplished, and by then Boone had seen enough to know that his idea was a success. White men could out-Indian an Indian. He was sitting on the ground with his horse's reins draped over his arm when the Irish sergeant prodded up the seven remaining prisoners. In the background came his troopers; not in any order of squads, but slouching up as individual fighting men, with pride shining in their faces. They came silently, for they wore moccasins, and they came dirty and sweaty and triumphant. He greeted them frankly and honestly.

"You could lick any soldiers the general could put in the field, boys, and here's the proof. Live Dakotas and damned well beaten ones." He looked at the sergeant. "Casualties, Sergeant?"

The Irish eyes flashed in the wet light of a late half-moon. "None, Sir. Not a damned one. Two horses wounded is all, and they're Injun horses at that."

"How many horses?"

"Not counting the two hit ones, we got thirty."

Boone's smile widened. "Well — that's part of your pay. I've got the general's word on that. You're in charge of sellin' 'em, Sergeant. Whatever you get from the emigrants around the fort you split among the men. I don't want any of it. This," he motioned toward them all, the staring, shiny-eyed Dakotas included, "is my reward. He turned to the first Indian. "You a Brulé?"

"Oglala," the man said.

Boone asked no more. He got up and flexed his legs and motioned toward his men. "Let's go back. Some of you boys tie these bucks on horses and watch 'em like hawks. They're slippery as the devil."

They struck out with herdsmen driving the captured, painted and decorated Indian horses ahead of them. It was a spectacle to make any army man stop and stare, for some of Boone's irregulars had appropriated eagle feathers in honour of their first 'coup,' and had the things stuck at varying angles into their campaign hats. Besides, there was no order. Men rode together and in little groups, lagged back and rode ahead. Only with the horses and the prisoners were there any seriously occupied and orderly troopers, and here there were many, for the prisoners were their first trophies and the horses were their extra dividend.

They rode back into Fort Laramie in the late afternoon, took the startled stares of their fellows and friends in stride, and turned their captives over to the guard-house officer, then corraled their Indian horses. Boone swung down before Captain Porter's office and grinned at the officers who stood on the duckboards watching the wild, undisciplined Indians and their just as independent captors. Captain Porter stepped down into the dust and went over to where Boone stood hipshot watching his men disband. By that time every man had an eagle feather stuck jauntily in his campaign hat.

"Good Lord," the heavy officer said, "I never saw such — such . . ."

"Disreputable looking regular army soldiers," Boone finished for him, then he laughed aloud. "Nor have I, Captain, but you'll always be able to tell my men from yours. By the feathers. That's an Indian custom they weren't long in adopting. I hope to hell it isn't the last thing they learn from their enemies, either."

Porter's black beard parted and he smiled wryly, shaking his head as he did so. "Damndest bunch I ever saw. Tell me what happened."

Boone did, omitting no detail. There was natural and ringing pride in his voice. He had to repeat the story firsthand for the general, when the post grape-vine got around to informing the commandant what had happened. But the third time he told it was by far the most rewarding. That was when Jane fed him a large supper and laughed with him, her face flushed from cooking and her eyes brimming with pride for her man. That was the best time of all. Boone wound it all up when he drank his coffee and she settled back by the fire beside him.

"What will you do next, Boone?"

He looked over at her with the satisfaction patently in his expression. "We'll hunt up some more, but what I want is a really big war party. Brulés under Red Calf. I want to hurt them so badly they'll stay away. Raid farther away over in their own hunting country. Either that or I want to manoeuvre them so's they'll come in where I can steer the army onto them. Honey — I want to bring 'em to heel as far as the country around Laramie's concerned. Do you understand?"

"Yes," she said. "I understand, Boone. I understood that when you were training the men, and I want it to be like that, too."

He leaned over against her. "It's hard on you, isn't it?"

She looked swiftly at his profile, turned slowly and nodded into the reflection from the fireplace. "Yes, it's hard on any wife, Boone. It's hard on me just like it is on the others."

He reached up and pulled her down to him. She felt like she had, once before to

208

him; heavier. He considered it for a moment, then decided against commenting on it, and held her close with a long, bearish hug, and kissed her. "Well — maybe we'll get our wish one of these days. I think we will, Jane. I think they'll make the mistake of coming in to fight. I hope so. I hope it with all my heart, because then, we can make it safe for the others — like us — who want to make claims and build homes out here."

"I hope it comes soon. But I hope it comes without the risk — without the danger. I'm afraid of that."

He nodded into her glance and bent his head, and kissed her.

Chapter Six

HOKA-HEY!

The snow was light although the winter was well advanced. It had been heavier but a chinook had melted a lot of it by the time Boone requisitioned paniers of grain from the quartermaster and led his men out again. Bundled in blankets with only their arms free, Boone's rangers looked more Indian than ever. He forgave them their strutting too, although the other troopers around the fort didn't. He overlooked their failings because he was leading them into suffering. He had devised a new strategy and wanted to try it out.

Always before, the Indians holed-up during the hard winters. Being nomads, they put up no horse fodder nor grew any grain for their animals. To keep their shivering horses alive they either herded them where the cottonwoods grew or cut soft-bark logs and dragged them where the animals could eat them. Indian horses in winter were rarely strong enough to carry warring riders. Boone was riding a government animal, big and fat and powerful, and he had taken with him nothing but the precious grain. His men had to ride light, carrying only their arms and blankets. All other pack space in the paniers was used for horse rations.

Scouts went ahead to break the trail and make for the ridges where they'd sit for hours, looking for the thin blades of village smoke that arose straight up toward the grey, forbidding overcast. The land was white — eye-searing white — as far as a man could see. The Dakotas were out there whiling away the winter, some place, and Boone wanted to find them.

He plodded, blue-lipped, through the below-zero weather in a great arc around the Fort Laramie country. Twice he passed over the ground he had filed a claim to, and once he even made his camp in the ruin of the old Barlow house. That night there were ghosts sitting with him and he hardly spoke. The men left him alone.

The days went past slowly, greyly, with short light hours and long black ones, building up into dismal weeks that were hushed in the brittleness of the winter grip. Finally a scout brought back word of a

Northern Cheyenne village huddled under the lee-side of a cutbank along a little meandering creek.

"How many lodges?"

The scout shrugged. "Hard to say, but I'd reckon 'em to be abount sixty, maybe eighty, in number."

"You didn't count 'em?" Boone asked the man with a frosty look.

"Sure, we counted all we dared, but there's a slew of 'em under that cutbank an' if we'd got that close, they'd a seen us."

"Oh. 'You locate the horse herd?"

"Yeah. I left a man watching near the herd and another keeping an eye on the camp. 'We going to hit it?"

"You're damned right," Boone said, then he turned and beckoned the Irish sergeant over. "Let's head for those trees yonder. You've heard about the Cheyenne village?"

The sergeant smiled thinly. "I've heard," he said. "Same strategy?"

Boone bobbed his head and struck out for a clump of snow-bent pines on their right, a half a mile or so away. The band followed him and swung down, all but the scouts who faced him with solemn looks. "You boys scout 'em and get it all set in your minds, then come on back. Watch for hunters," he added as an afterthought, then he turned and motioned toward the pack animals. The soldiers went to work taking off the pack-outfits, graining the horses, and lugging the paniers to a little protected spot where a spin-drift of snow lay, and put them where they'd be dry. The sergeant came up and grinned into Boone's face.

"Any ideas, Boone?"

Boone dropped down and offered a bag of jerky from which he was eating. "Hard to say until the scouts come back, but if it's like they say — the Indians under the cutbank — we may not have too much trouble over it. Stampede their horses first, if we can, then surround the village and come in shooting from all sides."

"How many bucks'd be in eighty lodges, Boone?"

"Well — mostly they figure two bucks to a tent, Searg, but I've always sort of held that one was a closer figure."

The Irishman's blue eyes shot wide open and he swallowed. "You mean there's somewhere around a hundred warriors down there?"

Boone nodded and chewed blandly, offering the jerky bag again without looking into the officer's astonished face. "I reckon," he said laconically.

The sergeant took a strip of jerky and held it in his hand apparently forgetting he had it. "Pretty damned big odds," he said softly.

"Yeah." Then he explained about the weak, starved and bony Indian horses. "That's our hope, Sergeant. We'll attack the village. Ride in from all sides and sweep on through, re-form and sweep back through again. The horse thieves will go in first, like before, but this time I'd just as soon see the Indians get to their horses. I want to test my idea about this winter skirmishing."

"All right," the little Irishman said, looking down, seeing the jerky in his hand and raising it to his mouth. "I'll line out the thieves first, then pass the word for the surround. That all?"

"All," Boone said with one short nod. There were a dozen other things in his mind but nothing that he could speak of at that moment. He sat hunched over, watching the little Irishman saunter among the other rangers. The sergeant showed none of his original astonishment when he went among the enlisted troopers. Instead, he acted bland and quite matter-of-fact about the approximate number of hostiles.

When the scouts came back one of them

214

held his hand up, palm forward, fingers closed, and Boone got up, walked to his horse and saddled up. His example was the order. The others went to their animals and began throwing up saddles. Mounted, the entire band rode closer. Boone waited. When they were close around him he briefed them again, then told them what was to come after the fight — if they came off victorious, only he didn't say it like that. He spoke as though there could only be one outcome.

"Their women and children will scatter. Let 'em go and let the old people go. The bucks'll try to get to their horses and whether they do or not won't make much difference. The fighting will probably centralise around the fleeing Cheyennes — the women and kids and oldsters — they'll try to make a line between us and them. Let them. What we want is the village. When they're all out in the snow fighting a rearguard action to protect their people, I want you to burn that village. I want it completely demolished — understand?"

No one spoke. No one had to. Boone turned away and led them. Far out in the snow was a scout sitting his horse. He was facing them, watching. When Boone was close enough he nodded to the soldier, then swung and nodded again to the sergeant who in turn swung his arm aloft, made a circling motion and brought the arm down in a forward thrust that pointed toward the hidden village under the cutbank ahead of them a quarter of a mile or so. Riders swung away from the main group and rode at a slow lope off to the southwest where another scout sat, beckoning them in. The horse thieves were on their way. Their guide was waiting for them. Boone watched them come together, merge and pause, then turn and ride almost due west behind the man who had scouted out the Cheyenne horse herd. His heart was full. It showed in his face when he smiled. He turned and caught the stare of a young, dark-skinned trooper, full on him.

"Scairt?"

The trooper shook his head. "No," he said. "I was just sittin' here wonderin' why the Army never used men like this."

The sergeant's chuckle answered him. "That's easy, man," he said softly. "You aren't a man to the Army. You're part of a blue line."

Boone turned back and listened, heard nothing and raised his arm and dropped it, turned to find the nearest scout and nodded to the man. The band fanned out a little, staying behind the scout who was showing them the way down into the little valley where the Indians were.

They were going down a trodden path, inches deep in icy slush, when somewhere along the conical lodges ahead a shout echoed back to them. Boone looked up quickly and saw Indians appearing from the tipis. Some had only their blankets snugged up close against the cold, more curious than alarmed, while others — obviously warriors — clutched either rifles or bows. For a terrible, unbelieving second, the Northern Cheyennes stood and stared. They were thunderstruck. By a sort of enforced truce, neither side did much fighting during the awful winter months, and yet there, fanning out in a great thin circle, were white men in blue uniforms. True, most of them wore coup-feathers and none of them looked as spotless as blue-bellies ordinarily looked, but one could see their pale faces. They were soldiers all right.

The cries began in fright and swelled to anger and defiance. The sharp, small sound of gunfire came to Boone. He ignored it, watching his men going through the early afternoon shadows. Then the

Cheyennes poured out and milled, crying out in confusion and astonishment for wasted moments while Boone's rangers closed their circle and stood in their stirrups, riding towards them in a howling, carbine-waving, loosely formed circle. When the Indians broke and ran just as Boone had known they would, the women dragged along children too small to keep up and too large to carry. Dogs ran in among them barking and howling, being fallen over and kicked at. The colourful throng seemed to unravel, come apart and break over into individuals.

The firing was thunderous. Only one thing was louder; the drum-roll throbbing of the frozen earth under the powerful hooves of Helm's Rangers. Boone had scornfully discarded the cavalry saber as an unnecessary accoutrement, and wisely, too, for rarely indeed did Indians stand before a concerted charge of mounted soldliers. Now, the white men loomed large, their faces distorted with their screams and their horses' eyes rolling and red with the gunsmoke smell and the frantic bedlam.

Into the camp they swept, knocking over and riding down what few fighting Cheyennes stood their ground. The noise was a deafening welter of hideous screams. Then the horsemen were past, their horses blowing and veering in toward one another until the circle was no more and the men, wild-eyed, sweating and crawling with raw nerve-ends, swerved around and spurred over into another belly-down charge that swept through the Cheyenne village the second time.

Boone hauled back on his reins. The big government horse slid, flinging dirty snow high into the air. "The village, boys — save nothing. Burn it and every damn thing in it!" He bellowed at the sergeant and waved his arm. All but ten or fifteen men followed him. The others swung down and shouted to one another, triumph showing in their faces.

Boone watched the Indians forming ahead of him to repulse the whites. Badly outnumbered, Boone's men never had time to worry about it. They had the offensive and carried it with them, charging toward the stubbornly retreating, badly mauled Indians until they were within rifle range, then Boone reined up and held his arm aloft. When the troopers gathered in close, he stood in his stirrups and pointed to their enemies.

"There they are, boys," he shouted.

"Take a good look. They outnumber you two to one, and they're running, you're not. Remember that next time someone tells you we've got to outnumber them to win. And remember something else your Army doesn't know. You don't have to kill their kids and wives to lick 'em. You don't even have to lick the warriors. All you have to do is to get their horses and force them out of their villages — in the wintertime. That's all. Now — let's get back and destroy their village."

The Cheyenne fighting men had stopped and straightened up. They were watching Helm's Rangers without moving or speaking — or comprehending either. The rangers turned their backs and loped back towards their village — then the Indians understood. A long dismal wail went up from them and many broke away, racing over where the pony herd had been.

But it was useless. Boone's men loaded their saddlebags with pemmican and jerky, with buffalo guts of hoarded fat, and with all the withered, unappetising but wonderfully nutritious dried food they could. Aside from that, however, they took nothing. Boone showed them the way in destruction. His mouth was a drawn line and his eyes were bitter. He emptied stored fat on to the piles of robes and war bonnets, fringed clothing and ceremonial rugs, tipi hides and saddles, and set it all afire. He shot holes in iron kettles and left nothing of any use whatsoever behind. Every man of his rangers followed suit until a few Cheyennes, who had ridden in closer or stalked back, shivering and afoot, cried out in terrible grief against the awful destruction. When their cries were the loudest, Boone raised up and motioned his men away.

They mounted and rode back the way they had come, very slowly, for the Indians — the bravest, hardest fighting Indians of all the Plains Tribesmen — the Fighting Cheyennes — were all around them.

Up on the plateau above the cutbank, the Indian horses were being driven in a wild circle by the scouts. It wasn't hard to exhaust the animals. They were little more than hair and bone and hide. Boone swung his gaze slowly, and saw the specks that were fleeing Cheyenne women dotting the snow for miles and a thick, round billow of black smoke that arose from below the plateau. A segment of mounted Cheyennes was riding towards them. There weren't many, but there were enough. They were caricatures of what they had looked like in the warm summers of "greasy grass" when their horses were fat.

"Maybe thirty, forty of 'em," the sergeant said, speculatively. "Look at t'em horses. Gawd . . ."

The Indians came in a slow, painful walk. Boone watched, and when they were near enough he heard them as well. They were chanting dirges. His attention was drawn away by a sudden, ragged volley of gunfire from over near the rim of the hidden canyon. There was a black clutch of advancing Indians over there. Afoot and all but naked, they nevertheless had guns and bows among them. They too were coming to fight. Boone watched both parties approach and pulled his mouth down.

"The ones on foot can't hurt us. The ones a-horseback are just about afoot. That's something else for you boys to remember. In the wintertime, if you've got a fat horse and a little grain, you can ride rings round an In'yun. Now — you're going to learn something else. We're not going to fight them. That's the way they do it. That's the way we're going to do it. Come on." He turned his horse and rode slowly away.

Almost immediately the Cheyennes who were afoot raised the yell. Boone reined up, twisted and looked back at them. They were waving for him to come back and fight. Not all the hand signals said that. Some were more personal, more insulting and obscene. He took off his hat and waved it back to them. A ripple of hard laughter went among his men. They rode on and didn't turn again until the mounted hostiles yelled their wail calls and kicked up their scarecrow horses, then Boone stopped and watched them coming. He had a tight little squint up around his eyes. Sitting like that, he waited until the Cheyennes were as close as he wanted them, then he turned and led his men away from the pursuers with only a little effort. The Indian horses couldn't begin to overtake their foemen and the bitter harangues died out as the distance between the two parties widened and lengthened.

Boone didn't ride hard, but he rode long until the shroud of freezing night was all around them like a white shelter and only the oily smell of the desolation they were riding away from clung to their nostrils.

And later, when he and the sergeant were huddled over a smoky fire that hissed constantly with wet wood, Boone was satisfied that his theory had been perfectly sound. He ate jerky and drank snow-water coffee and felt good inside. The news of the disaster his rangers had inflicted would reach every Indian raiding in the southern country. He wanted it to be like that. He also knew that in time the story would find its way to Fort Laramie, and he wanted that too, because he had no intention whatsoever of returning to the fort now, like he usually did after a successful campaign.

"Colder 'n a Dakota's heart," the little sergeant said with a rueful grin.

"That's what we want, Searg. We want it to stay cold like this. We want the Indian horses to stay poor and weak until we've finished our circle around the Laramie country. I want to break them this winter and scatter and destroy 'em so badly they'll never come down here again."

The Irishman's face steadied at Boone's vehemence. He regarded his commander thoughtfully but was far too wise to ask questions. Not right then, when Boone's eyes shone like blue ice in the ghostly night. He looked down suddenly and poked at the little cooking fire with a damp twig. "We've got half a circle made."

Boone answered the Irishman's unspoken question when next he spoke. "And we'll make it tight all around before we go back, too."

The sergeant sighed under his breath, drained off the last of his coffee and lay back in his newly acquired, wild smelling buffalo bedrobe, and looked up at the brittle stars that blinked angrily, coldly, down at him. Sometimes a man went through a lot over a bunch of . . . well . . . maybe it was like Boone Helm said. People should be raising something out of all this rich ground, not spilling their blood and guts over it forever and getting back nothing but trouble and more trouble. Still — it was warm back at the post. He fell asleep thinking like that, unaware that the brooding profile of Boone's face, with its broad chin and too-prominent cheekbones, fell across his chest.

Boone sat hunched over the fire, smoking, looking into the black distance and seeing nothing but old ghosts and new ideas that merged into a world of his own making, where he was wise-man and war-leader, both.

There were all the old memories there in the night with him, Parker Ellis and Tyre Barlow and Jane. He remembered how she had looked when he had first seen her that wild night in the smoky glow of the lantern coming in among the Dakota captives. He thought back to the days of Conquering Bear, of that long winter with Little Thunder's band, of all the people he had known who were no more, both Red and white. Then he looked out over the little bivouac of sprawled men and into the blackness beyond, where the sentinels were.

Few men wanted to kill, no wise men did, but there was no choice and it wasn't altogether the fault of the Red men. Yet in order to create order and security out of the havoc wrought by both sides, he had to kill if he wanted the life for himself, for his wife and the children he wanted to have, and that was that.

He slept after the others were rising up, here and there, to relieve the guards. He didn't dream although the breath of victory was in him very strongly. When he awakened the troopers had eaten and stood beside their saddled, freshly grained horses. He motioned them in around him and spoke frankly, watching their expressions.

"Boys — what we did yesterday was a terrible thing. Maybe I know it better than you because I've lived with Indians. But it had to be done like that. We beat them the only way they can be really beaten. We had to set them afoot. Now they're helpless and the winter will do what we didn't finish. They'll have to go back up north and live with the Dakotas, or hunt up another Cheyenne encampment and move in there.

"But — if you're feeling guilty — remember this. We killed no women and children and we left them their guns and bows. They'll suffer plenty, but they won't starve." He stopped there, peering into their faces, with the dirt-grime and whisker-stubble. "I want you to know that what we've done is necessary. You may not like it — I don't, I'll tell you — but it's necessary. Do you understand?"

The men spoke all at once, making a dull, hard rumble of incoherent sound, then the Irish sergeant spoke over the other voices.

"Hell, Boone — we know how you feel and understand all right — only — we don't feel the same way, altogether. Those damned hostiles've been killing soldiers too long. Not a man here as hasn't seen a friend killed. If you'd o' said the word, we'd o' scrubbed every damned one o' 'em out. That's how we feel, so you don't have to apologise."

"No," Boone said slowly, "we're not out

to kill their women and kids. The best way to humble 'em — to beat the fight out of 'em — is the way we did it yesterday. Well — let's ride. Swing southwest and make our big circle. Maybe we can run down a few more. I think we've pretty well convinced 'em this country down here's a bad place to live in, and that's what we want 'em to believe."

They rode slowly, hunched over, into the teeth of a savage wind that blew into their faces relentlessly. They beat their way due south so as to offset the wind-burn a lot, then, after two days of torture the wind died away as suddenly as it had come up and a deceptive, mild warmth took its place. As they swung east, Boone cocked his head a little, every once in a while, and studied the high overcast. The dark pregnant belly of sky was swollen and lowering and sinister looking.

"I don't like this, Sergeant. Don't like the smell of it. There's going to be a hell of a storm."

The Irishman shot a squinty stare skywards. "Looks bad," he said. "No question about it. Is there any cover hereabouts? Hate like hell to get froze to death, but I'd hate it worse without a little shelter."

Boone rolled his head and studied the snowy world they were riding over. Familiar landmarks were covered over with a deceptive whiteness that looked beautiful and soft, and actually was death with a white shroud on. But he knew this country, summer or winter. It was always the same, barring the white colour. "Yes, I think we can make it to the Buckhorn. There's a creek about thirty miles from here."

"Shelter down there?" the sergeant asked in a voice a little hoarse.

"Well," Boone replied, "there's willows and some cottonwoods there. No houses and the like, but we can make wickiups. How's the grain holding out?"

"We got enough to last weeks yet. It'll burn 'em out eventually, though."

Boone looked back at their horses. The animals showed the hard usage all right, but they had plenty of spring in their steps yet. He lowered his nose into the funnel of cloth he'd tied around his throat and rode on in silence. If they made the Buckhorn they'd be all right — barring a blizzard like had ice-locked the land the same year Parker Ellis had gone over to the Dakotas. He held his mind from dwelling on his old pardner, but a bile-taste of bitterness seeped through him just the same until he

229

swore, making jerky streamers of frosty breath in the still air. He thought there wasn't much chance of Parker Ellis, the renegade, being anywhere around a white man's fort. Old Park'd watch that all right. Every fort and outpost had a gaunt scaffold for men who turned against their own people. There weren't many, and of those few even less were ever caught, but the gibbets remained just the same.

Buckhorn Creek was a sluggish little trickle of water in the hot times of the year and a white ribbon of glass-like ice in the winter. It was thickly defined by the tangles of willows and great, fat cottonwoods that lined it as far as a man could see, up and down country. Nearing the place, Boone sent the scouts on ahead in a routine patrol to seek out game and to look for a good protected area for their camp. He was riding in sombre silence with his under-officer beside him like a diminutive lump of robed and blanketed shapelessness, thinking of his hutment back at the fort and his wife, when the sergeant's head came up quickly. Boone saw the abrupt motion out of the corner of his eye. He used a fist previously hidden under the mound of warm covering he wore to rub away the hoarfrost around his eyes, and he slitted them against the snow-glare.

One scout was plodding back alone. Boone reined up so suddenly that the man behind him cursed and hauled back. Boone heard and ignored the sound. The scout came on, a strip of buffalo hide under his decrepit campaign hat tied tightly under his chin, making an incongruous and ridiculous sight, but no one noticed it then. Not when one scout came back to the column alone. That had a significance they all understood very well. Indians!

The man used no prelude. He jumped right into the middle of his thoughts and spoke them curtly. "Indians up ahead. Hell of a big band of 'em. Lord — they got lance stands set up right out there in the snow. It's a warrior party, I'll lay odds on't."

Boone was shocked. By his rough estimate they weren't far from the fort. Buckhorn Creek, in fact, wandered right across the section of land adjoining the old Barlow place, that he'd recently acquired title to. "How many lodges?" His voice sounded un-real in the lowering stillness that was terrifying in itself, unless one was used to it.

"Slew of 'em, Boone," the scout said

with a solemn look from beneath his old hat. "We didn't count 'em. No time — you boys was movin' up too fast. Another hour an' you'd ridden right into 'em." The man cuffed frost off his scraggly, unkempt beard. "I'd guess at least a hundred lodges."

Boone heard the sergeant's quick intake of breath and ignored that too. He didn't hesitate with his answer. "Too many. If it was a village like that Cheyenne town, that'd be different. But a hundred *akicita* lodges — that means nothing but fighting bucks. We wouldn't stand a chance."

The scout made a crooked smile. His eyes were sardonic in the pinched ugliness of his bluish face. "We come out to find 'em an' fight 'em," he said quietly, never dropping his glance.

Boone said nothing for a moment, then he shrugged with a harsh white line showing above his upper lip. "Well — Searg — what do you say?"

The Irishman looked at Boone in surprise. It showed in his eyes like high flags flying. "Gawd — over a hundred Dog Soldiers. We'd be outnumbered to hell and back."

Boone turned back to the scout. "Are they Northern Cheyenne or Dakotas?"

"Both, from the signs on the tipis. Irish is right — they've got Dog Soldiers with 'em. We seen the symbols on the tents."

Boone sat silently again, looking beyond the scout's shoulders into the white vacuum. Dog Soldiers — the fightingest warrior-society of the fightingest Indians on the Plains. It could be the end of every one of them, for, once engaged, there would be no retreat. Dog Soldiers were master strategists. If they could get Boone's command surrounded, that would mean the end of them all. They never asked nor gave quarter. He squinted harder, until his face was all drawn up below the eyes, and the eyes themselves nearly closed.

"We've got three advantages, boys. Our horses, the fact that we know where they are and they don't imagine a white soldier's within twenty miles of 'em — and a way of fighting they've never seen white men use before." He turned to the sergeant. "Well, Irish — you reckon that makes us near enough to equal — or not?"

The conflicting emotions tumbled over the under-officer's face in a riot of confusion, until finally he wagged his head. "I'm scairt to say, Boone. For myself — well — all right. I'll ride where ye lead, boy. But for the men — it's their lives."

Boone nodded stonily and flicked a hand aft. "Ride down the line and ask 'em. I'll wait."

"Boone, if we whipped this bunch — that'd about end it — wouldn't it?"

"Maybe," he said answering the scout. "Depends on who they are. With Northern Cheyennes and Dakotas — hell — with all Indians, just one thing counts. Prestige. Whoever's the biggest and the greatest and has the most coups. Well — if this is a big leader's war party, an' we make 'em eat crow — that'd just about convince the rest of the hostiles it's not safe down here."

The scout sat his horse and listened, then spoke into the silence that was broken only by a buzzing among the men behind Boone. "There's some pretty big medicine lads down there, I'd guess. There's one lodge pretty close to where I come over the hill that's got a big white eagle painted on its side. I reckon that one's a pretty hot leader."

Boone didn't hear the words. They ran on and on, like water falling over mossy rocks, blurred and indistinct and unheard in anything but the drone.

Wambdi Ska. White Eagle. Red Calf had called Parker Ellis that. Oh — God — no.

Not Park. He wouldn't do that. Boone raised his head and stared at the scout and saw him sharply in the reflection of his own turmoil. "Tell me about this lodge with the white eagle on it." He listened to the description of the other animals — the symbols painted boldly around the white eagle — and his breath came short and hard before he nodded his head and stopped the drawling voice. "That's enough. That's — plenty."

The scout was regarding him strangely, with bright, unblinking eyes, when the sergeant rode up and reined in beside Boone and spoke into the aura of sick-shock that lay over the commander, without sensing it at all. His face was flushed.

"The boys say 'let's have at 'em.' That's good enough for me, Boone. They got a lot o' horses. With what we already got, it could mean a lot o' money for us."

The silence lengthened, with both the scout and the Irishman looking oddly at their commander. "Boone?" the sergeant said. "Did you hear me?"

"Yes. Thanks, Irish. Fine — well — let's study the thing out a bit."

He sat there listening as the men went over the plans, withdrawn and stony looking. If a man might be said to age in a matter of hours, Boone did. When the under-officer asked questions he answered in a flat voice, but he answered, and eventually he fought out of the pall that had so strangely engulfed him and looked into the cold, hard-eyed faces, and took his part in the council.

"We've got to make full use of two things. Our strong horses against their weak ones, and the fact that we'll surprise the devil out of 'em. But — you're in for the goddamndest fight of your lives, believe me. Not just with the Dakotas, boys, but with the Cheyenne Dog Soldiers. I'll tell you what I believe. I believe they're the greatest fighting society in the country." His sunken eyes gleamed at them. "Not just out here on the frontier — boys — but in the whole country."

He was conscious of the close look he was getting from the sergeant. "Don't get off your horses for anything. If they're shot out from under you, find another one quick and stay up on it. Afoot, they'll cut you to pieces. You're good, boys — damned good — but you're going up against the best there is, out there, and I want it stuck in your heads that what I say now, is so."

He stopped and studied the reaction to

his words. The expressions were mixed, but it was soul-satisfying to him to see that the doubts were negligible before the resolution that far out-numbered them. Then he nodded his head at them all. "It'll be dark shortly. I think we'd better lie over until just before dawn. It'll be the coldest then, and they'll be asleep. We've got to take every advantage. Remember — it'll be close to three to one."

"But — gawd —," one man said. "We'll be nigh froze by dawn."

Boone looked savagely at them. "Sleep with your guns next to your skin, boys. Don't let any frost or snow get near 'em. That's all that's going to give us victory; those guns, our horses — and surprise. Fight like you've never dreamed of fighting. If you don't, I give you my word — you'll never fight again."

After that he went back into the silences. There was a darkly forbidding look to him that they all saw and wondered about. It was still there, ground into his rigid, weathered face when the sergeant hunkered beside him and chewed jerky in the gathering gloom.

"I sent word out to the scouts," he said softly, matter-of-factly, avoiding looking at the bleak face there beside him in the still hushed world. "They'll come in and pass around what they know just before dawn. Others'll take over. That way everybody'll know the way things are down there."

Boone heard the soft words and looked up, saw the thinness of the face with its weather beaten lines. "Searg — you're wondering. All right, I'll tell you. There's a white man down there among them. The tent with the white eagle on it is his. You'd call him a renegade. To you, he is. To me — I knew him a long time; rode and hunted and trapped and lived with him. Well — you wouldn't look at things like he does. Neither would I, but I understand why he does — and you don't." He raised his arm as though to ward off something, then let it drop.

"Maybe you've seen pardners killed by Indians. I don't know — but — did you ever know one was going to be killed because he wouldn't have it any other way — wouldn't let himself be taken alive — and have to sit there — here — and remember all those other times?"

The Irishman didn't answer. Two bright, dark red splotches of colour showed high in his face below the eyes and his jaw muscles were set in an unforgiving bulge. Boone saw, and understood that, too. He

238

dropped his glance to the dirty snow at his feet and spoke so quietly that, except for the awful hush of the night, the words would have been lost.

"A cow, that first time, three horses the next time — and this — so men can live in safety — raise kids — die and be buried in their own land."

The sergeant didn't move for a long time, then he got up and without speaking, walked away and went over among the men and rolled into his buffalo robe. He lay there in the blackness, feeling the storm that was brooding above them, watching the humped-over figure by the fire, not knowing what to think except that a white renegade was down there. He had to die; must die.

Boone Helm was a good man, a strong man, and a wise leader — but this was different. The Irishman's eyes were hooded. He lay a long time dry-eyed and slash-mouthed with his jaw muscles locked. This was something else and no man could ever make him think differently about it. Not even Boone, whom he admired above all men.

Boone didn't sleep and after a while he dug the little parfleche bag out from under his robe and ate the stringy-tough meat and felt a lot better. There was a kind of numbness somewhere behind his eyes that sealed off the dagger-pain. He chewed slowly, methodically, because jerky requires a lot of chewing, and turned his mind to the other things that were imminent and perilous and seemed to thicken around the little bivouac. The greyness deepened, became deathly still and brittle-cold and black, then gradually, draggingly, began to lighten ever so little with the piled up mass of a lowering sky the colour of dead flesh.

He had wanted just what lay ahead; a fight that would end the Indian wars around the Laramie country. A chance to inflict such a smashing, terrible defeat upon the Dakotas and their allies that no fighting warriors would consider the risk worth the plunder, in the southern plains again.

Dog Soldiers were the most ferocious of all Plains soldier-societies, and down in the protective willows of Buckhorn Creek was a war party of them. Why were they there, this time of the year? He mulled it over and gave it up. Beyond the elemental reason of an attack — perhaps a flaming series of stunning blows across the frozen belly of this, their old land — there could be no reason. And yet — he chewed and thought there had never been such a thing occur before.

It might be a good omen at that. If such a formidable and undoubtedly well-known excursion should be hopelessly shattered, beaten beyond all shadow of a doubt and sent back to the people in defeat, the end of the Sioux War in the Laramie country might be achieved.

He thought of this for a long time and knew he had to whip the Indians regardless of Dog Soldiers or Parker Ellis. Here was the opportunity he had vainly sought for so long. That Fate had dealt him the body-blow with his old friend's presence couldn't detract. It was ironic and anguishing — but it was so — and there it was.

He remembered the Sun Dance ceremonies they had sat and watched in the fragrant nights together. He recalled so many, many things; how Ellis had gradually changed; grown more silent, more bitter and morose. How his defection had come upon Boone with a stunning suddenness only because the younger man had been too engrossed to see and recognise the slow-coming symptoms. It took an effort to wrench his mind away from the vivid memories, but before he did it for the last time, he said a dolorous Dakota prayer — the kind Parker's new god would understand — then he made up a shorter, less poignant one in English, and said that too.

Then the scout came on sodden moccasins and touched his shoulder. The fingers were still. "Gettin' light, ain't it, Boone?"

A nod. "I reckon. Rouse up the sergeant, will you?"

The man didn't answer. He padded across the crisp snow with small, sharp sounds that told of the frozen crust over it. Boone was tucking away his jerky bag, making it fast with a thong to his belt when the Irishman hunkered beside him and looked at his face once, then kept his eyes on Boone's throat while they talked.

"Did I make it clear to 'em, not to dismount — no matter what happens?"

"I'm sure o' it."

"Well — it's time to send out the horsethieves. But this frost over the snow, Irish — it'll be a dead give-away."

"Anything they can do?"

"No. One advantage to hitting a war party over a village, under these conditions, they'll have no dogs to hear the boys coming and rouse the camp. They might have sentinels out, but I sort of think this bunch doesn't or they'd of prowled around here in the night. Well — when you send the thieves out, Irish, tell 'em to save their horses up until they're within sight of the herd — then make a run for it. It's the only thing they can do. Otherwise — someone's sure to be awake and hear 'em. We've got to keep the surprise — you understand?"

"Yes," the sergeant said, then paused and ran his tongue in a quick, furtive circuit of his lips. "Boone? That renegade down there." He said it like a question and left it there without amplification.

"Never mind him," Boone said. His mouth went closed with finality. The under-officer arose from his squat and nodded, shifted from one foot to the other, then turned abruptly and went into the huddle of waking men. Boone watched him go, arose and flexed cold-cramped legs, then struck out over the snow in scarch of his horse.

The animals were grained. They didn't seem to have suffered any from the biting cold and stood patiently, drowsy-eyed, waiting for whatever came next.

The men detailed to rout the Indian horses — called "horse thieves" by their companions — mounted stiffly and rode off single file. Boone watched them go thinking that they looked and acted like their enemies, and that was good, for it meant they had come to think almost like an Indian. It made his mouth curl up a little like a wolf's does when he walks away from a trap-set.

The horse thieves faded into the night with only the faint, brittle sounds of their passing lingering. Well — he had learned to think like an Indian, and now there were others he'd taught, doing the same thing.

The reward for it lay behind them all, in the record of their little troop, which rivaled and surpassed the records of whole blue-belly regiments.

"Boone? There's a scout in."

He turned and looked past the little Irishman at the hulking, wide-faced soldier behind him. Saw the man's blue-cold look and the fierceness in his flaring-out nostrils and sucked-flat mouth and remembered him from the training days. He waited until the scout spoke.

"The thieves just passed us out there where the land slopes down to the creek. Everything looks fine. We scouted 'm four ways an' couldn't find a guard. There must not be one."

"It's common enough," Boone said. "They're like us in that. When they're feeling plenty safe they don't bother putting out any." He looked at the sergeant but spoke to the scout. "Anything else?"

"No, just that ever' thing's ready — it looks like."

"Good. Searg — detail the boys. Into the camp like always, re-form and ride back. Set fire to the lodges if they can. Don't dismount no matter what — an' don't let 'em split the command up or surround it. Shoot to kill." He was turning toward his horse, gathering up the reins and toeing into the stirrup when he finished it. "No prisoners unless they come at you with their arms in the air and with no weapons showing." He swung up and looked down meaningly into the Irishman's face. "It better go off smooth and fast. You know what I mean, Sergeant."

"I understand," the little Irishman said simply, then he too turned to the horse-guards, sought out his mount and swung up. There was a strange, unbidden pathos in his heart that hadn't been there the night before. It irritated him to feel it now, when the imminence of unleashing his hatred against a renegade was approaching. He turned his horse and looked at Boone, saw the thick arm go up and come

245

down swiftly — with a clenched fist.

The sergeant wasn't the only one who reached surreptitiously beneath the thick body coverings and fingered an Angus Dei that was hidden and warm, suspended from its buckskin thong around a neck. They shook off all the little fealties and obstructions that possessed them and rode through the murky darkness with only the thought of what lay ahead, gripping every man-jack of them.

A Sioux word ran constantly through Boone's mind as he rode. *Hotam' itan'iu.* Dog Men. Dog Soldiers. Somewhere up ahead in the hush, was a war party of the deadliest fighters of the Plains. It made his stomach tighten with the chill of taut nerves. He had wanted an opportunity to beat the Dakotas forever away from Laramie, but he hadn't expected such an opportunity as this. He didn't want it now, but there it was, and if he should emerge triumphant, his mission would be accomplished. Against ordinary Dakotas and Northern Cheyennes — he had stood an excellent chance. Against Dog Soldiers . . . ?

He rode like an automaton and faced ahead with a blank, wooden expression — and there was honest fear in his chest, too, although it didn't show because he wouldn't let it; not even in the greyness of this half-world. There was something else as well. A churning that seemed more a fever of the flesh than of the spirit, but it wasn't of the flesh and he knew it. All the same it was tangible.

The land was just beginning to slope under his horse's hooves when he saw the conical, taper-tipis of the hostiles. They were hard to distinguish from the snow-shroud of the background land-swell and had an eerie camouflage lent them by the overall gloom. But they were down there, scattered indiscriminately like Dakota lodges usually were, with places for staked-out war horses to be kept handy. Boone studied the village and even before he found the white-eagle symbol, he saw something else that made the whole thing clear. In the distance was a large, blood red calf painted across the hide lodge of a strong leader whose house sat just a little aloof from the other lodges. Red Calf!

Boone looked for a long time at the symbol, then he smiled to himself. So the challenge he had cast at the feet of the warrior had been accepted. That was it. Red Calf had come back and brought his warrior-society and his allies. He was here to make Boone Helm eat crow. He may have even come this far with the intention of going farther. Down to Laramie, possibly, and count coup before the adobe walls, thus humbling the white man who had set him free.

A slow anger boiled in Boone. The Dakotas were here to show their wiliness by attacking white settlers when the deep snow was over the land. It would be a great surprise and unquestionably a great success — a Dakota raid like that in the middle of winter.

The sergeant squirmed in his saddle. Boone turned and the shine of his teeth was grey-white. "I hope the boys slept with their guns, Irish," he said.

"They did. No fear o'er that, Boone. They've learned well enough."

"Yeah," Boone said. "The thieves are taking a long time."

The under-officer swore with feeling. "They sure are. Makes a man's scalp crawl."

"Keep it up where it grew when it crawls like that, Sergeant, and you'll live to scare your grandchildren to death with stories like this one's going to be."

The sergeant blew on one stiff hand and held his reins with the other one. "Things like this'll keep me from havin' any grand-children," he said in a muted voice. "Lord, why don't they hurry up." Boone didn't move a muscle until the Irishman spoke again. "How many d'you think're down there, Boone?"

"Hundred and twenty, maybe. See that lodge with the red calf painted on it?"

"Yeah. Is that what the thing is? 'Been tryin' to guess what the drawer had in mind. Funny lookin' calf. What about it?"

"There's a big Dakota in there. He's called Red Calf. If you count coup on him I'll give you twenty dollars."

The Irishman forgot to blow on his knuckles while he fixed his eyes on the lodge set out a little apart. "You want to pay me now, just in case you don't — aren't able to pay me, later?"

Boone laughed softly and threw his head back in that way he had. "Collect it from my wife. She'll take your word for it."

The sergeant's glance never wavered from Red Calf's taper-tipi. Not even after he flexed his fingers, found them loose enough to grip his pistol, tugged the belt-gun from beneath his wrappings and hefted it.

Then the sound they had been waiting so impatiently for, came. The sharp barks of the horse thieves and the shrill, frightened nickering of panicked horses, and the scrambling, brittle sound of their running hooves.

Boone shot a last fast look at the silhouettes around him in the leaden world, saw the steady glint of metal and raised his arm, took in a great gulp of frozen air and slashed downward with his clenched fist and let out a roar.

"*Hoka-hey!* Charge!"

Chapter Seven

A NEW HORIZON

Simultaneously, with the eruption of Helm's Rangers over the lip of land down towards the Indian encampment, it began to snow, large, lazy flakes that fell softly. There was no wind with them. Just the world of silence broken by the shouts of the white men sweeping down toward the Dakota and Northern Cheyenne lodges, riding like dark wraiths a-horseback through a white world.

Boone saw the snow without heeding it. His pistol rode balanced in his fist and his eyes were slitted against the swept-back, icy air that struck his face and drove water out the corners of his eyes.

The rangers were almost upon the village before anyone appeared among the lodges. When the dark shadows came running out into the sub-zero weather they were almost naked or altogether naked, for the Indians slept raw summer or winter and in their puffy-eyed alarm they had thought only of grasping their weapons and charging out to face the threat that was in the greyness.

Deep-throated cries and a muffled bedlam of eeriness was all around them. Gunfire was muted too, adding to the ghostliness of the weird battle. Men dodged and lunged, fired and fell back before the horsemen. Boone was swept along into the very heart of the lodges and saw the astonishment in the dark faces that loomed up suddenly around him. He fired into the nearest targets and heard his own voice above the confusion.

The Indians fought without giving much ground. Some were knocked over by charging horsemen. Others knelt naked, notching in arrows and firing at the elusive targets all around them. Mounted men leaned far over to fire point-blank into the backs of Dog Soldiers.

It was a scene calculated to inspire a sense of unreality in the hearts of the white soldiers, and yet they were a part of it and fought with the same savagery as their enemies did. But the advantage lay with them, for the Indians were too startled, too completely caught unawares to do more than hunker and fight back defensively while the first wild rush of mounted men swung down upon them. Someone fired a tipi. As though reminded of a duty slighted, other horsemen rode in closer and leaned far out of their saddles to start more fires so that in a matter of terrible minutes, the heavy snowfall was made all the more unreal by tongues of flame.

Boone saw a tall Indian jump up and let out a mighty howl, then turn and race out into the near obscurity where the thickening snowfall obscured him almost instantly. Fearing what might happen if his rangers got out of sight of one another in that closing ring of whiteness, he rode frantically among them shouting for them to stay together. He found the sergeant bare-headed, mouth agape, panting and re-loading his pistol in the very midst of the macabre drama.

"Irish — don't let 'em follow the Indians. Too hard to see. Tell 'em to stay within sight o' one another."

"All right," the under-officer yelled back, then, as though it were of primary importance, he twisted up his face and yelled. "Look there — in front of you. You owe me twenty dollars."

Boone glanced down, puzzled, completely forgetting his officer until he saw the sprawled, grotesquely flat body of a big

Dakota, face up and very dead. Red Calf. He remembered then and looked around to nod. The sergeant was gone and the whirling battle had shifted to the outer edge of the village where the Indians were fighting off the savage attacks of their enemies and trying to make an orderly retreat toward where their horse herd had been — and was no more.

Boone nudged his horse toward the fight and dimly saw a rider sweep up beside him. He turned to look just as the man's horse gave a loud squeal of pain and rage and bogged its head, bucking as hard as he could. Watching, Boone saw the man's head snap back and his stirrups fly free, then, for a long second, the rider hung there in the air before he started to fall. Instinctively Boone swung toward the un-horsed soldier, yelled at the dazed man and reached down for him, felt his arm beneath his protective blanketing and gave a mighty heave. Stupefied from the fall, the man nevertheless responded with a jump and Boone flung him up behind him so that they were riding double. The soldier screamed something but it wasn't understandable in the racket and Boone spurred forward, up where his men were driving the Indians farther out into the snow. The ground was dotted with the dead, and twice riderless horses bumped them. The first one jerked wildly away from the rescued soldier's attempt to snatch its bridle. The man's cursing was plain enough until he had secured the second animal and swung himself astride it, then Boone reined away from him, never completely identifying the soldier he had rescued at all.

Someone lunged up beside him howling. It was the sergeant. He made a sweeping gesture that Boone understood and nodded repeatedly at, then the two of them rode into the forefront of their men and led the riders in a great charge through the stubborn line of warriors so that they flanked the Indians. The men twisted in their saddles and fired vindictively back at their foemen, then rode hard behind their leaders.

The steam of horse breath was like a twin muzzleblast all around them when they reined up out of sight of their enemies. As suddenly as the deafening clamour had started, it died away. Occasionally a shot came from the area of the burning village, but it was inspired by rage, not accuracy.

Boone looked back down toward the

creek, saw the vague, almost obscured glow of the fires and spoke in a panting way with the roar of his heated blood in his ears.

"Once more through 'em, boys. Don't lose sight o' the man next to you. This snow'll be against them just like it is for us. Drive 'em away from their village this time. Let 'em fall back where they think their horses are and keep 'em out there. Don't let 'em get back into the village at all."

"They'll surround us," the sergeant protested. "We're out-numbered."

Boone swore angrily. "Let 'em. They can surround us forever if they want to. If we can hold their village, the snow and freeze'll do our fighting for us. They're naked. They've got no food and no fire. Let 'em keep their damned surround all winter if they want to." Someone laughed irrationally, a high, spine-tingling sound that tore ragged edges along the thick shroud of hush they were sitting in.

Boone faced the Irishman. "Find the horse thieves. Lead 'em around behind the Indians and stampede the horse herd right over the red devils. They're worth a regiment of soldiers if you use 'em right. Then let the horses come right on into the village and the rest of us'll hold 'em there.

You boys follow through behind 'em; get in with us." He turned, breath spewing out of his parted lips like smoke. "All right? Let's go back!"

They did, sweeping floundering warriors before them. Evidently two thirds of the Indians had tried to find their horses. Failing that, some were trying to get back to the village through the deepening snow. A long, uneven ripple of gunfire came from the riders and warned the Indians they were returning. Cries of defiance rang through the increasing snowfall, but targets were elusive things. No man saw an enemy until he was almost on top of him and a serious failing was hampering the hostiles. Wet bow-strings, stiffening fingers, and the growing snowdrifts made it almost impossible for them to run and dodge away.

The light from the fires made a shrill, hissing sound that was loud enough to add a persistent crescendo to the abrupt explosion of other sounds; gunfire, shouts, wild cries of triumph, and death chants. The Indians had to give way before the formidable pressure of the mounted men. In order to try to equalise the overwhelming pressure of the white men — the *wasicuns* — the Indians concentrated on their horses. It drew off the murderous fire from the men, who in turn poured volley after volley into the Indians, forcing them to fall back in spite of themselves. The men who had their mounts shot from under them, formed a withering second rank of marksmen behind those still mounted. The fire of the unmounted men was more telling, more accurate and deadly, than the fire of the mounted men, whose accuracy at best was never too good, for the hurricane deck of an excited horse was indeed a poor shooting platform.

In spite of the heavy numbers opposing them, Boone Helm's men had consistently held to the offensive and the Indians never really had an opportunity to rally and attack. Driven away from their lodges, they sent murderous fusilades of musket ball and war-arrows through the thickening snowfall. Boone had finally dismounted, ordered his men to seek shelter among the tipis that still stood, or lie flat in the snow. The horse-guards were detailed ample protection and when the sergeant came up, stared in horror at his commander and spoke, and the first phase of the bitter fight was over.

"Lord, what happened to you? Does it hurt?"

Puzzled, Boone looked into the pinched, blue face of the Irishman with a scowl. "Does what hurt?"

"That," the sergeant said, pointing, "your head."

Boone ran an exploring hand over the side of his head. The shock was great when he felt the congealing blood up there. Examining the wound closer, he discovered that a war-arrow had torn the lobe of his ear to shreds, and yet there was no clear recollection in his mind of when the near-escape had happened. He shook his head.

"I'll be damned. 'Didn't know it happened. There's no feeling there. Well —," he turned away and dropped his bloody fingers to his side, "we've whittled down the odds. Go among the boys, Irish, and tell 'em to lie low and keep a close look. The hostiles may try to storm the place. It's that or freeze to death, for them. Tell 'em too, that if we lose the village we're goners. Detail 'em in relays. Lyin' in the snow's their best chance to avoid bein' hit." He glanced into the snow cramped near-distance. "This is going to be one hell of a storm. We might wind up sitting out the winter here." He thought back to another time, years back, when he'd been

snow-bound in an Indian encampment —
and that brought another thought, too.
"Keep a sharp watch, Sergeant, and stay
right with the boys. This is the crucial part
of the battle, remember that."

He was still speaking in bursts of short-
ened breath, the steam rising above his
bloody looking face with the edging of
frost on it, when they heard the shrill barks
of the horse thieves over the other noises.
Both men stood transfixed and motionless,
their faces turned into the snowfall that
beat against their skin like tiny fists of
white.

The noise swelled until the Dakota and
Cheyenne gunfire died almost completely,
then a long, dismal wail arose and was
muffled, as though it came from a great
distance. One cry above the others was
repeated over and over, taken up by the
doubled over, badly shattered and freezing
tribesmen. It was coming closer, too.

"Fight no more," they were crying out.
"Fight no more!"

Boone watched them coming toward the
village with arms above their heads, their
coppery bodies showing a tightness caused
by the awful cold. He swung an arm as he
called out to the sergeant.

"Keep 'em out there. Don't let 'em get

in among the lodges. Strip 'em — every damned one; they'll have hidden knives and pistols."

The sergeant looked dumbfounded. "Boone! They're surrendering!"

"I know. They hear the horse herd coming behind 'em. They think it's more soldiers. Send scouts out to stop the horse thieves and hold the horses back until we can get 'em all under guard. Hurry!"

And that was what it was. Boone's idea of having the stolen Indian horses stampeded through the warriors from their rear had worked out, ironically enough, so that the Indians thought the rumble of the great body of animals behind them was more troops. They surrendered on the strength of that thought. Boone's irregulars were just as dumbfounded as he and the sergeant. Even after the sergeant shouted orders to them and they were obeying them, stripping the humbled Dog Soldiers and Dakotas, making a pile of their weapons in the deep snow and herding them apart and guarding them, they still were astonished at the sudden capitulation of the superior Indian fighting force.

The camp was a ghost-village of men, Red and white, separated and humped over against the blizzard's force, by the time order was established and the horse-thieves had driven their charges in among the willowbreaks along the frozen-over creek. The sergeant had the remaining lodges systematically plundered of robes, blankets and food. These were apportioned among the miserables with the lion's share going to Helm's Rangers. A large medicine lodge was turned into a hospital tent, kept warm with a dry-wood fire.

The men lived out the storm which lasted three terrible days. Then, miraculously, the sun came out with blinding intensity, as though determined to ameliorate the agony caused by the storm. The men really weren't much better off. Aside from the rivulets that ran everywhere, making walking a nightmare of discomfort, their eyes couldn't adjust quickly enough to the abrupt change and watered greatly.

But before the sun had made it possible for men and animals to travel again, Boone had followed up the vagrant thought he'd had the day the hostiles surrendered. He went into the lodge with the big white eagle painted on it, bending low to enter the door-hole and felt the warmth inside. Across the little fire that arose from the fire-hole in the center of the tipi a man sat, rocking a little, bundled in a buffalo robe, staring into the fire and ignoring everything else.

"Parker —."

The man's head came up. His eyes were so sunken that the fire's shadow showed them deeply recessed in the lined, weathered caricature of his face. He said nothing.

Boone let the flap fall behind him, crossed to the fire and lowered himself, facing the door. He was surprised to find Parker Ellis in there — and yet not really, either. Something deep inside him said he'd find his old pardner there. There had been a blood-track in the snow path outside . . .

"It's all over, Parker."

"I know." The voice was soft, like a stray, lost breeze through the high treetops in autumn. "I saw it."

"Why did you go with them?"

"No choice, Boone. I told them it was bad. They said if I was a Dakota I should prove it. I came along."

Boone thought back to old man Garnier; remembered how the Indians had accepted him for years, then, in their irrational, frenzied way, had turned on him only because they were wild with fury at the whites.

They had killed him and hacked him to pieces with their knives — just because he was the only available white man.

"I told you they'd do that, Parker."

"I didn't believe it," the slow, tight voice said. Ellis didn't move once. His glance stayed on the hypnotically swaying, bright little tongues of flame.

Boone felt the stifling warmth of the lodge. It wasn't really that close inside, but his blood was still coursing fast. There was acid-sweat on his body. "What were they going to do?"

"Count coup. Red Calf — you challenged him. He brought them back to make you eat crow. They were going to show . . ."

"I guessed that."

The howling wind came up and worried the naked lodge poles that protruded above the smoke-hole, then just as suddenly died away with a sobbing sound.

Boone reached up and felt the torn ear lobe. The thing was swollen but not bleeding. He rubbed at the dried blood with an annoyed insistence. "You want to know how I did it, Parker?"

The older man shook his head slowly, logily. "No," he said, "you did it, that's all that matters. It's all over — I saw that before I came back in here."

"You were in the fight? I didn't see you."

"Yes, I was there. You wouldn't have recognised me anyway. My war shirt —," he said, and then said no more.

"With the Dakotas, Parker?"

"Yes, you know that."

Boone sat there wondering how to say what came next and steeled himself for the task. But the words wouldn't shape up except with a brutality he particularly didn't want them to have. He sweated — and then he never had to say them. Parker Ellis began to fall forward before Boone caught the movement out of the corner of his eye, and by that time his astonishment was overcome enough for him to reach out and grasp the tightly held buffalo robe and pull mightily to keep the older man from falling across the little fire, Parker Ellis was dead.

He sat there without moving, staring into the upturned, white face, strangely drained of blood, and saw death in the still, unseeing eyes. While he was staring, the sergeant pushed through the door-hole and blinked at them, then he let the flap fall behind him and straightened up, looking down at Parker Ellis. Boone said nothing, hardly knowing the little officer was there in the lodge with him until he began to speak in a quiet, stilted way.

"I wondered about him, Boone. I meant to tell you about it. It happened hours ago. I saw this man — he had a rifle with him and wouldn't retreat with the others. I shot at him twice. Missed the first time but the second time he was turning away and the ball broke his rifle. It — almost knocked him down. He turned and looked at me — then — it was the damndest thing I ever saw — but I could see his eyes. They weren't black an' I knew he wasn't no Injun. Figured he was this renegade. Before I could get my pistol out — this man flung back his robe, took out a big knife and — looking right at me, Boone, he ripped himself across the belly. God — I never seen . . . Then he dropped the knife, pulled the robe up around him an' walked over here to this lodge. I didn't have time to hunt him up — not until right now. That's why I come in here — now — to see . . ."

Boone was reaching down at the folds of the tightly clasped robe. He had to loosen Parker Ellis' fingers from it. When he lifted it he saw what the sergeant said was true, and put the robe back over the horrible wound that Ellis had sat there hiding, rocking a little, when Boone had first come in.

Boone got up very slowly. There was a terrible tiredness in him and stiffness as well. He didn't look into the sergeant's face at all, but avoided it and jutted his chin, Indian fashion, toward the door-hole.

"Send squads of the In'yuns along the creek. Guard 'em heavy, and have 'em cut bundles of fire wood — enough for every In'yun to carry on his back. Then line 'em out an' we'll start for home."

"Through this snow?" the sergeant asked.

"Through this snow," Boone said. "And send their four strongest warriors in here to me."

The little Irishman stood silently, knowing there would be more. He didn't find the atmosphere pleasant nor Boone's face good to look upon either, but he waited.

"Send a detail on ahead. Tell 'em to fetch back soldiers. The boys can't sleep with all these prisoners — and they need rest. Let the Army do a little. Tell 'em to tell Porter we want a big escort sent back and fast."

"All right."

"And one more thing. You remember that deserted log-house we camped at and I told you about one time? The Barlow Place?"

"Yes."

"Well — set our course so's we'll camp there."

"All right, Boone."

"There're shovels there," Boone said absently. "Maybe the ground won't be frozen over either."

Mystified but wise enough not to ask questions, the sergeant went back out. Boone waited until the Indians came, then he motioned toward the body of Parker Ellis. "Wrap him and carry him among you."

The column left the ruined encampment with its grim reminders of the fierce engagement lying frozen in the snow. They carried the seven dead soldiers while the eighteen wounded rode either astride with Boone's column or were borne in buffalo-robe litters. The sun held despite the massing of clouds off to the north and the mushy ground underfoot didn't add anything to the discomfort of their passing; it couldn't.

Two days of difficult travel, then the old house of Tyre Barlow was ahead, its gaping doorway a reminder of the earlier tragedy, and there they met the relief column from Laramie. There, also, Boone had the sergeant put the prisoners to digging a deep narrow grave beside where Tyre Barlow lay. Parker Ellis was wrapped in his robes and buried there. Boone had two medicine-men give an Indian eulogy and ceremony above the hard, dark earth, then he himself said what had been in his mind for two days. It wasn't exactly a prayer; it was more of an apology to the white man's God for the man who lay in the ground at his feet. And after that he went back to the officer-tent and presented himself. There wasn't much to say, and he said it bluntly. The Army listened and asked a few questions — not many because it was plain Boone Helm had no intention of answering very many. After that, his rangers lay down around their fires and slept. They dropped over the edge of the known world into a dark abyss of oblivion so deep that even with the noise of the Army getting under way for its trip back to Fort Laramie with the bedraggled Northern Cheyenne and Dakota prisoners, didn't awaken them. Only Boone, the Irish sergeant and two sentinels, saw them go like herded cattle ahead of the soldiers.

Boone's men used up an entire day resting. They gorged on the white man's food the Army had brought. They slept until they could sleep no more, then drank coffee and talked among themselves, and very gradually, Boone was drawn back into their circle. When they finally struck out on the final trail back, he was almost as he had been before. Riding beside the under-officer, he was tactfully reminded of the twenty dollar bounty by the presentation of Red Calf's scalp — duly fleshed out and stretched within the little twig circlet, the hair ornaments still intact. He paid up and motioned away the trophy.

"You keep it, Irish. I won't ever need any reminders of this scrap."

The sergeant tucked the trophy back into a scuffed saddlebag. "Did we do it, Boone? Do you think they'll come down here again?"

Boone shook his head and kept his eyes on the bold outline of the fort far ahead. "No, not after they hear what happened to the war party. Oh — there may be raids every now and then, but they won't amount to much. In a little time, there won't even be those. We did it, Irish. Look — the gates're open."

The sergeant's squint swung toward the

fort. He smiled a little. "Goin' to be a regular reception, Boone. Look there's the band."

The musie came wonderfully to them and Boone smiled at the sight of the cold soldiers lined up, watching their approach. He thought privately that those garrison troops would be swearing under their breaths at being ordered out like that. Then he laughed. It was a sound of relief. He had won. He had achieved exactly what he'd wanted to achieve. There was a solid sense of victory, but no feeling of triumph at all. Just the knowledge . . .

Captain Porter took his careless salute and hustled him through the throng of soldiers to the general's office where the commandant stood and held out his hand. They shook and the general nodded toward a chair. Boone sat, waiting.

"You've shown us something, Mister Helm, and we're grateful. I want you to know that even the President —," here, the general picked up a paper that had fold streaks in it, and lay it before Boone, who didn't look at it at all, "has sent his congratulations and a commendation. Of course — after that — my own personal commendation isn't worth much, but I offer it anyway along with my best congratulations. You've done a wonderful job with those men. Done it better than anyone ever dreamed it could be done."

"Thanks," Boone said. "I don't think they'll come down here any more. At least not for a long time."

"We're convinced of it," the commandant said. "Boone — you've been gone five months — do you realise that?"

Boone nodded. "Yes, I've kept track of time. It's been a long trip. The boys are tired and so am I. I want to resign my job with you now, general. I've done what I wanted to do."

The commanding officer's eyes widened. "Resign? Why — man — I've an offer here on my desk for your appointment to the rank of major in the regular army."

"I don't want it," Boone said quickly, almost harshly. "I am resigning right now. The sergeant can take over my scouts, but I'm through."

"Oh," the general said, "you've seen your wife already, then. Is that it?"

"No, not yet. She's part of my desire to quit, but mostly I just want to develop a claim I have. Make us a home — finally."

"Will you remain on the regimental books as an interpreter, then?"

"Yes, but only providin' it doesn't take

up too much of my time."

"Done," the general said, arising. "I'm sorry you won't take the commission though. Now — maybe you'd better go see your wife."

He left the hutment and went past the orderly and the guards outside without any more than noticing them. He crossed the parade to his own hutment and was startled to find two guards stationed, one on either side of the door. Then he went in and smelled the close warmth of the place — and a peculiar odour he had never smelt in their house; a strange, disconcerting . . .

"Boone! Oh darling — darling!"

She was sitting in front of the fireplace with an older woman. He went forward and knelt to kiss her, felt movement in the bundle in her lap and looked down with a shattering realisation of why she hadn't run to him like she always had before, and thrown herself into his arms.

"Here's your son, Boone. He's your image, darling."

Words wouldn't come and he forgot entirely the woman who was watching them, tears streaming down her face.

Jane reached up and touched his torn, healing ear. There was a fearful look far back in her eyes. Boone lifted one hand

and looked under the blanket at the wizened, flushed little face and let the blanket drop back, felt around for an arm of a chair, found the thing and let himself down into it with a wavering sense of weakness in his legs.

"Jane — I wondered — back, before we left. You were . . . Honey, when was he born?"

"A month ago," she said. "Boone, is it all over? Can we make our home now?"

He nodded. The happiness burst inside of him and even the sadness seemed without its grief. "What've you named him?"

She smiled. "I haven't, but I thought you'd want him named after you."

"No," he said quietly. "Let's call him Parker Tyre Helm."

Her smile stayed but mellowed a little, and she nodded at him. "I thought of that too, darling. I thought you might want it like that. That's why I didn't have him christened."

He leaned back in the chair and regarded her with a long quiet look. There was a sort of ponderous, solemn happiness in the look, "God is good," he said. She understood perfectly, for God *was* good . . .

We hope you have enjoyed this Large Print book. Other Thorndike Press or Chivers Press Large Print books are available at your library or directly from the publishers.

For more information about current and upcoming titles, please call or write, without obligation, to:

Thorndike Press
295 Kennedy Memorial Drive
Waterville, ME 04901
Tel. (800) 223-1244
Tel. (800) 223-6121

OR

Chivers Press Limited
Windsor Bridge Road
Bath BA2 3AX
England
Tel. (0225) 335336

All our Large Print titles are designed for easy reading, and all our books are made to last.